MW01643818

RONT MATTER

C *hromatic Mirage*

In the electric midnight, neon dreams ignite,
'here every heartbeat pulses with a riot of light.
ıadows shimmer in hues of vivid fire,
nleashing secrets in a dazzling, bold choir.
vibrant maze of truth and fierce desire—
eality fractures into luminous, untamed fire.

ena Lexington March 2025 Bangkok

YPNOTIZED ASSASSIN/A Gripping Psychological rime Thriller

y Lena Lexington

opyright

edication

r those who dare to question the unseen,
r the restless minds that chase the shadows,
nd for every soul that fights to reclaim its own truth.

cknowledgments

HYPNOTIZED ASSASSIN

A Gripping Psychological Crime Thriller

Lena Lexington

Table of Contents

This book is a tribute to the relentless pursuit of truth and the power of the human mind. My heartfelt thanks to family, friends, and every reader who has inspired and supported me on this journey. Your belief in stories that challenge conventions and explore the depths of psychology has been my guiding light.

Preface

In a world where the line between reality and nightmare blurs, *Hypnotized Assassin* invites you into the labyrinth of a troubled mind. Dr. Miranda Carter, a renowned forensic psychologist, finds herself ensnared in a series of brutal sleepwalking murders—cases that force her to confront not only a chilling global conspiracy but also the darkest corners of her own past.

What begins as an investigation into inexplicable crimes soon unravels a tapestry of mind control, erased memories, and a government experiment known only as Project Morpheus. As the clues lead Miranda through a maze of deception, she is forced to question: Was she merely a bystander, or the very key to a deadly program that turns ordinary people into killers?

This is a story of psychological warfare, of hidden agendas lurking in the shadows, and of a woman fighting against an invisible force determined to control her destiny. Prepare yourself for a journey that challenges your perceptions, blurs the boundaries of free will, and leaves you pondering the true nature of identity.

Echoes in the Shadows- Share Your Thoughts

Thank you for joining me on this dark, twisted journey through *Hypnotized Assassin* . If the novel captivated you, challenged your perceptions, or left you pondering long after the final page, I invite you to share your thoughts. Your honest review not only helps shape future works but also guides fellow readers in discovering this story. Please take a moment to leave a review and let your voice be heard. Your feedback is deeply appreciated.

INTRODUCTION

Step into a world where the boundaries between dreams and reality shatter like fragile glass under the weight of forbidden secrets. *Hypnotized Assassin* is not merely a crime thriller—it's an electrifying journey into the depths of the human psyche, where every shadow hides a story and every heartbeat reverberates with mystery.

In the midst of this dark labyrinth, Dr. Miranda Carter, a brilliant forensic psychologist, finds herself ensnared in a web of chilling sleepwalking murders and global conspiracies. As forgotten memories resurface and a sinister government experiment resurges, Miranda must confront the haunting possibility that the enemy lies not only in the shadows—but within herself.

Prepare to be captivated by a narrative that pulses with vibrant energy and relentless suspense. With every page, let the neon glow of intrigue illuminate your path through a maze of deception, mind control, and unforeseen twists. If you're ready to have your perceptions challenged and your imagination ignited, dive into *Hypnotized Assassin* —where the night is alive with secrets, and every moment holds the promise of revelation.

Chapter 1

The First Awakening

The Sleepwalker's Nightmare

Daniel Hayes wakes to the rust-tinged smell of iron. Consciousness creeps in like a slow-rolling fog, the realization dragging him from the depth of sleep into the stark light of morning horror. The sheets beneath him cling, sodden and sticky. He blinks hard, trying to shake the grog of night from his vision, but what lingers when his eyes finally focus steals his breath away.

A muffled scream chokes him, rushing air running hollow through his throat as he stares at his wife. Her unmoving silhouette, dappled in deep crimson, conjures memories of sunsets they once shared. But this sky is blood-soaked, the artist unbidden, his medium dark and cruel.

A trembling hand gropes for the phone, the world narrowing to the frantic beating of his heart and the cool weight of the device as he stumbles through an emergency dial. His fingers move with all the precision of a man tethered by strings pulled from above, his voice a tapestry of fear and confusion when the dispatcher answers.

"I didn't—I don't remember," he stammers, articulation fractured by ragged breaths. He barely registers the assuring cadence on the other end, his mind spinning, wheels unhinged from their track. He can offer no narrative beyond the muted horror reflected in his wide eyes, the dwindling certainty in his grip.

As the call ends and reality sinks its teeth deeper, Daniel stumbles to his feet, his movements mechanical, driven by raw panic and an overwhelming urge to flee even his own skin. He paces through the monochrome expanse of his apartment, where no evidence of the night's chaos reveals itself beyond his own stained flesh and the silent voice of his absent memory.

The police arrive with a swiftness that jars him further from coherence. Officers, solemn and scrutinizing, flow through the apartment like a murmuration, their practiced examination a dance of methodical calm cloaked in whispered urgency. They explore every untouched corner and unruffled surface, seeking the tapestry of struggle that would transform his words from lies to truth. But their search yields no such gift.

"Sir, you need to come with us now," an officer intones, his grip firm against Daniel's elbow, steering him gently yet insistently from the scene of his waking torment. Daniel's feet shuffle, each step a mile, his gaze casting half-formed pleas at the indifference of walls and windows.

"I was asleep," he insists, the alarm of the words growing hollow in his ears with every repetition. It is a mantra now, an incantation against the threat of his own blank slate memory and the invisible ink written in his dreams.

The gravity of silence envelops the apartment as they usher him out, the spaces they leave behind echoing only with abscncc. A numbing vacancy overwhelms where laughter used to stand; empty now, save for questions without answers and a gnawing dread that it may be all he ever retrieves from the depth of his hidden mind.

Miranda's Introduction

Dr. Miranda Carter pushes through the bustling city streets of New York, the chill of the early morning air brushing against her cheeks as she approaches the address. It's one of those pristine, modern apartment buildings with glass facades reflecting the drama of the city back at itself. She fits the key into the lock, feeling the slightest tremor in her hand—a residue of doubt she hopes won't show.

As soon as she steps into the building, Detective Alex Reed is already there, his figure a silhouette in the dimly lit corridor. His eyes, shadowed by weariness, scan her approach with the indifferent precision of a seasoned investigator. He offers a nod, merely a formality, before diving straight into the case.

"They say it's sleepwalking." Reed's voice carries a note of skepticism as he relays the situation outside the apartment door. "An unusual defense for a murder this brutal, don't you think?"

Miranda absorbs his words, a sense of unease threading through her thoughts. The defense is not unheard of; cases with somnambulistic violence have dotted her career, yet they were riddled with complexities that tested her understanding. She wonders if, once again, the intricacies will mirror her own past lapses, moments where her own insights felt insufficient. This case, she fears, might be one of those times that will push her to the edge of her expertise, where every word carries the weight of a potential misstep. These high-stakes investigations often flirt with the thin line between failure and victory—she's balanced there before, felt the thrill and the threat of it. Yet, beneath the surface of her composure, an old fear stirs: the fear of failing to see clearly, of misjudging the depths of deception that might lie ahead.

Reed gestures for her to follow him inside. "No sign of a struggle, no forced entry," he continues, his stride confident as they thread through the solemn rooms. "The husband swears he was asleep. Something doesn't add up."

Miranda's gaze sweeps over the stark scene, the piercing white walls and minimalist decor now marked by grim reality. The absence of struggle gnaws at her. Quietly, she moves through the room, assessing each piece of furniture, each shadowed corner. Reed's doubts resonate within her, mingling with her own uncertainty—a blend of instinct and inquiry that churns relentlessly beneath her calm façade.

Together, they step deeper into the apartment's silence, each step accompanied by the soft crunch of broken glass underfoot, a sharp reminder of the chaos not long past. Her pen dances across her notebook, capturing details in tidy, precise scripts. Each mark represents a bridge between chaos and clarity—a testament to her intent to uncover what lies beneath the polished veneer of the apartment.

Their conversation ebbs as they absorb their surroundings, the distant hum of the city life filtering through the high-rise windows. Miranda places her focus intently on Reed, trying to discern a measure of his instincts. She wants to trust his insight, to lean into a growing partnership that challenges her guarded, instinctual solitude. And yet, her own analysis whispers caution, pulling her focus back to the task, reminding her that true understanding requires her own unwavering conviction.

Outside these walls, life continues unchecked—another morning teeming with idle chatter and business as usual. But here, a chilling serenity dominates. The juxtaposition is stark, a jolt that sharpens her senses as she resolves to unravel the mysteries surrounding this case, knowing all too well that some shadows can extend far and deep, unexpectedly entwining with her own.

The Detective's Skepticism

The forensic lights cast harsh patterns over the apartment as Detective Alex Reed stands amidst the stark reality of Daniel Hayes's alleged crime. The metallic scent of blood lingers in the air, mixing with the currents of a night unearthed, as technicians buzz around the scene. His brow furrows, deep in thought, with skepticism tugging at his every observation.

Reed turns to Dr. Miranda Carter, who stands beside him, her eyes scanning every detail with clinical precision. "Sleepwalking, huh?" His tone is skeptical, almost incredulous, as the words linger between them like an open question. "Convenient defense for a guy who wakes up next to his dead wife."

Miranda continues her quiet assessment, cataloging the absence of forced entry or signs of a struggle. Her voice is calm, laden with the weight of expertise. "Sleep disorders can be complex, Detective. There are cases where actions during sleepwalking episodes have led to harm." She jots down her observations, the click of her pen the only sound breaking their conversation.

"Complex or not, you're asking me to believe that someone can just... do this in their sleep?" Reed gestures broadly to the scene around them, disbelief edging his words. "I read people, Miranda. And I'm not one to buy into convenient excuses."

Miranda pauses, choosing her words carefully. Her demeanor remains composed, even as tension brews between their clashing perspectives. "There are triggers, psychological and physiological, that can manifest in sleepwalking behaviors. Nocturnal dissociation can make the improbable possible, regardless of how it seems."

Their conversation intensifies, each note of skepticism met with professionalism. Reed stands firm in his conviction that there's more lurking beneath the surface of this case, while Miranda's grounded explanations reflect dedication to understanding. Both are unwavering, yet their dialogue carves a rift—a silent challenge of intellects and motivations.

"I just can't help but think we need something more than science to untangle this mess," says Reed, leaning back slightly against the precinct wall, arms crossed. His eyes meet Miranda's, simmering with a mixture of doubt and curiosity that mirrors the brewing storm outside. "Because right now, Hayes's story is all we've got, and it's not enough."

Miranda nods, a silent agreement resting between them, acknowledging the vast chasm yet to be explored. As they conclude at the crime scene and step into the precinct's muted corridors, the echoes of their discussion linger—unresolved questions fueling the path ahead. Reed contemplates the missing pieces, the puzzle far from complete, and the case waits, steeped in shadows and hidden truths.

Unexplained Déjà Vu

The precinct buzzes with the kind of quiet tension that only a place committed to solving crimes can embody. Under the fluorescent lights, Detective Reed's voice punctures the air as Daniel Hayes begins his halting explanation, insisting that sleepwalking has stolen his consciousness and left chaos in its wake. Dr. Miranda Carter stands at the periphery of the discussion, her hands methodically flipping through pages of notes scribbled with her careful hand. Beneath her composed exterior, a storm of discomfort brews.

As Daniel speaks, each word seems to pull an invisible thread within her mind. His tale of unconscious brutality unravels a piece of her past she has no clear recollection of, yet it gnaws relentlessly at the edges of her awareness. It's the sort of déjà vu that isn't easily shaken, one that leaves a lingering fingerprint on the mind and stirs a deep-seated anxiety she struggles to articulate. She leans into her instincts, knowing they are rarely wrong, yet finding herself nearly undone by their implications.

Miranda attempts to refocus, grounding herself in the present by questioning the plausibility of Daniel's narrative. She is a scientist, after all—trained to separate emotion from fact. But the deja vu clings to her thoughts like a shadow, creating a persistent disorientation akin to being awoken from a deep sleep. Throughout the conversation, fragments of memories tease the corners of her consciousness, hinting at something unresolved—a link bypassing logical reasoning but thriving in the depths of intuition. Despite her best efforts, the unease festers, sparking with every glance she steals at the bloodstained walls of Daniel's predicament mirrored in her own expression.

With a painstaking thoroughness, she delves into her notes, cataloging every observation and aligning it with her unshakeable hunch that the past has come to haunt her. Her fingers press into the paper with each stroke of the pen, as if willing the act of writing to crystallize her swirling thoughts. The darkness given life in Daniel Hayes's account is compelling, hauntingly so—a visceral reflection of something buried deep within her. She wonders if her own history, the pieces of which she's labored to reconstruct over the years, might hold the key to both Daniel's and her unraveling.

Reed's analytical skepticism cuts through the noise in her head. "Miranda," he urges, a note of impatience curled around her name. "You think this sleepwalking story is airtight?"

She shakes the fog from her thoughts, meeting his gaze with newfound resilience. "In all my years, I've learned that the mind does extraordinary things, Alex. Even the most bizarre tales can hold a shard of truth," she replies, her tone calm yet tinged with an edge sharpened by her inner turmoil.

Reed's skepticism remains unhidden. "Truth or no, we've got a crime scene that tells a different story. We need facts, not feelings."

His words settle into the heavy air between them. Despite their disparate approaches, their paths align toward a shared objective—understanding the costs of Hayden's nocturnal escapades. Miranda knows her unease must be corralled, turned into momentum as they peer past the chaos toward clarity. She's driven by more than the immediate question of guilt or innocence. She's chasing an understanding that transcends Daniel's narrative, one that might reconnect the jigsawed pieces of her own identity—or fracture them permanently. Determined, Miranda clings to this pursuit, trusting her instincts despite the precariousness with which they lead her forward.

A Link to the Past

The precinct buzzes with the low murmur of officers and the rhythmic tap of keyboards, a backdrop to Miranda's focused task. She sits hunched over her workstation, scouring through a digital labyrinth of medical records. Her fingers swiftly navigate the keyboard, driven by an urgency that simmers beneath her composed exterior. Then, she stumbles onto a discovery that halts her motions—a record tied to Daniel Hayes. The notation reads: patient of the now-defunct sleep therapy clinic. Her curiosity flares, igniting a spark that prompts her to dig deeper into the clinic's shadowed past.

The Clinic of Somnus, the records say, was nestled inconspicuously within a bland industrial part of town, its façade indifferent to the extraordinary promises that once resided within. Yet, her probing reveals that the promises were laced with peril, as whispers of experimental treatments and ethical oversteps snake through archived articles and obscure forums. Her heart beats a bit faster; the facility was shuttered abruptly, leaving a vacuum filled with unanswered questions and a vague sense of deceit.

Miranda's breath hitches as an abrupt migraine grips her temples, a throbbing intrusion that demands her attention. It pulsates with an intensity that feels almost alive, stirring memories that lurk on the fringes of her consciousness. Brief, fragmented flashes assault her mind: blinding white lights, muffled voices, and the cool clinical sterility of an examination room. She's driven back to the screen, determined to uncover the clinic's cursed blueprint and its ties to Daniel Hayes.

In the quiet sanctum of the precinct's research office, a gnawing dread melds with her resolve. An image crystalizes in the facets of her mind—a recollection perhaps, of The Clinic of Somnus. It begins as a half-formed thought, a shimmering mirage that dances just beyond her reach. Yet within that elusive veil lies a truth too stark to ignore, a truth that might very well tether her own fragmented past to the harrowing crimes unfolding. There's a weight of knowing, the sombre awareness that perhaps her journey into unraveling this case will lead to the very core of her being.

Observations transmute into purpose. The residual ache from her migraine echoes in her thoughts as she shifts her focus from identification to intervention. She ponders the implications of Project Morpheus, a specter rising from the covert shadows of Cold War subterfuge—its jagged history woven into the fabric of national security and moral ambiguity. In the precinct's quiet recesses, she contemplates the delicate balance between moral duty and hidden truths, her responsibilities suspended under the swinging pendulum of ethical compromise.

“I need to know more about this clinic,” she scribbles a quick note, the words punching through the silence like footsteps in snow. Her gaze steadies on the computer, map lit by the cold luminescence of the screen. Determination alights in her eyes—a resolve tempered by the knowledge of dark corners yet unexplored.

The steady glow from her computer tenderly bathes Miranda’s features, casting a subtle play of light and shadow—a modern chiaroscuro that mirrors her credence. Her focus sharpens, a clear path emerging through the fog of misbegotten experiments and lost memories. She resolves to unravel this somnambulant conspiracy, knowing full well the specters she might awaken. Yet, in this moment of clarity, there’s no place for fear, only a plan to pierce through the shroud of deception wrapped around The Clinic of Somnus.

The First Puzzle Piece

The news conference at the precinct is a whirlwind of chaos and apprehension. Reporters clutch microphones like lifelines, hovering beneath the harsh glare of fluorescent lights that cast stark shadows over the room. Dr. Miranda Carter steps in, flanked by Detective Reed. Her posture is taut, reflecting the tension that has become a constant companion since the day she was thrust into this confounding series of events.

"The second murder follows an identical pattern to the first," announces a poised official at the podium, projecting a voice straining against the mounting unease. "We confirm the victim in Berlin was indeed linked to the same defunct sleep clinic as Daniel Hayes."

The revelation hangs in the air like an ominous fog. Miranda absorbs the details, her mind contorting with possibilities, the ever-present undercurrent of dread tugging at her resolve. The suggestion of a conspiracy sprawling across continents adds a chilling depth to her fears. Her instincts whisper that these mere threads of information barely scratch the surface of a plot far grander, and darker, than she had ever imagined.

Beside her, Reed leans slightly, murmuring into her ear, "This is getting out of hand. If there's a coordinated effort behind these murders, we might be dealing with a global operation."

Miranda nods, her expression a canvas of thought lines and anxiety. "It's bigger than we thought, Alex. We're not chasing ghosts; we're combating an elusive, systemic menace." Her voice is hoarse, burdened with knowledge and the weight of the paths they must tread.

Reed's skepticism teeters on the edge of his own curiosity and disbelief. "We have to tread carefully. This isn't just local law enforcement territory anymore." His eyes scan the room, gauging the reaction of their peers and the media assembly.

Miranda meets his gaze, her mind racing through a million scenarios. Each revelation, like a key in a lock, aligns an intricate puzzle, leading to more questions than answers. As she reflects on the broader implications of the murders, an unsettling reality begins to surface. The activation of sleeper agents could tear apart global stability, unleash chaos in diplomatic circles, and intertwine innocent lives in webs of violence. And yet, the wider populace remains oblivious, blissfully unaware of the dangers playing puppet master with the world's balance.

A subtle tremble grows within her, not just as an investigator unveiling a hidden conspiracy, but as a woman haunted by her entwined history with it. Memories claw through the depths of her mind, writhing specters of her own darkness. If the clinic held her memory's key, what part of these machinations might have insidiously been hers? She contemplates how easily one could be manipulated, an unwilling participant in a symphony of chaos.

The world may be blind to the existential threats lurking beneath polished smiles and diplomatic handshakes, but Miranda can't afford such ignorance. She is determined to peel back every layer, no matter how painful.

Press cameras flicker like a constant drizzle of stars, absorbing every nuance of expression shared between her and Reed. Their alliance, initially built on collaboration, now rests on the precarious edge of trust forged in shared danger. The polished veneer of professionalism masks the looming specter of doubt, yet they cling to a fragile thread of emerging understanding.

"We need to sync our efforts," Reed says finally, his voice steady against the din of rising voices. "This is more than just isolated incidents. We might have to stretch beyond our jurisdiction." His eyes lock with hers, weaving a subtle promise amid the chaos.

Miranda nods, a mutual realization cementing their resolve. All around, the precinct transforms into a symphony of anxious chatter and hurried footsteps. The world has only crested the brink of uncovering a veiled truth, and it demands more than vigilance—it demands audacity. Miranda clutches her notes as they exit the room, the weight of their unyielding quest for truth pressing down on her shoulders. In silence, she resolves to push further, recklessly if necessary, into the opaque abyss of this conspiracy.

A reporter's shouted question hangs in hollow echoes as the door swings shut behind them, sealing the withering tension within its metallic grip. The promise of answers sprawls beyond in the uncertainty of shadows and international ramifications, as vast and unfathomable as the night.

CHAPTER 2

THE SECOND KILLING

Another Sleepwalker?

The day breaks over Berlin with an ominous elegance. A gilded sun paints the cityscape, but its warmth fails to penetrate the cold opulence of the diplomat's apartment, where shadows cling stubbornly to corners. The morning light streams through expansive windows, revealing a sprawling scene of chaos and stillness intertwined. The body of the diplomat lies crumpled, life snuffed out in this haven of culture and power. Beneath the polished veneer of his life, the whispers of old secrets flutter like trapped birds.

Officials murmur in subdued tones, faces etched with the gravity of discovery. They comb through the ornate rooms, unearthing curious connections hinting at something more insidious—a trail back to a sleep clinic now marred by scandal. The whispered phrase "sleepwalker" flits through the air, echoing eerily like the tremor left behind by a ghost.

As the news barrels headlong into the digital bloodstream of the world, televisions buzz with animated fervor. Anchors speak in measured urgency, broadcasting the tragedy to strangers entwined in daily rituals continents away. Amongst ear-splitting sirens and clattering wheels, a fragmented alarm pierces the calm of Manhattan where the real world feels distant and dispirited.

Miranda Carter, cocooned within the sterile walls of her New York apartment, watches the chaos unravel on her screen. The newscast dances in reflection on her green eyes, while her hand clutches the phone, listening with a mind tethered to the past and a heart yearning for understanding.

"Miranda, this is turning into something monumental. We've got another sleepwalking situation, but this time it’s a diplomat. His connections—" Detective Reed's voice crackles with static urgency through the line, weaving swiftly past formalities in favor of connection.

"Where? Berlin, you said?" Her voice maintains an outer calm that her rapidly beating heart betrays. Another name marked by the shadows of Morpheus. Another journey into the darkness that her past refuses to relinquish.

"Yes, enough matches to your New York case that I’m hoping you can lend us your insight. There's more at play here than we’ve yet seen." His tone is as steady as her own, yet Miranda detects an undercurrent—a desire for resolution mingled with professional duty—but she cannot access this with certainty.

Quietly, Miranda continues to absorb the details Reed lays before her, mind churning with the implications. Each thread he unravels holds potential to tie her even deeper into a web she did not weave but is inexorably caught within. The world had believed Morpheus a specter long banished—a sinister experiment sequestered to the past. Yet ghosts resurface and governments tremble, each act a reminder of the hidden networks pulsing beneath the contrived calm of global diplomacy.

As Reed speaks, Miranda reflects on the world she wished to step away from. The heavy agony of her own history thickens the air around her, becoming something tangible. A profound fatigue drapes her shoulders; every decision shapes the form of her future yet tightens the chains of her past. The mere thought of returning willingly to that world—to be deployed yet again, an asset measured by the failures she might avert—pains her with a piercing clarity.

"Alright, then. I'll catch the first flight out," she agrees, the burden of the choice mapped into the tension constricting her voice. The line disconnects, and for a moment, Miranda stands suspended between realities as the Berlin skyline weaves itself into shadows upon her thoughts. She closes her eyes, steeling herself for the path that, though perilous, still beckons with whispered promises of justice.

Miranda swallows hard, returning the phone to its cradle. She allows herself one final, faltering breath before heading to pack. With each step setting her anchor deeper in shifting sands, she knows the past she flees will not release her until its echoes have had their say. An unfinished symphony, drawing her into the melody of unanswered questions—and somehow, she admits, that knowledge is both burden and relief. The worry remains etched across her face, clear and unwavering, suggesting that somewhere beyond the immediate, lies a truth waiting to be told.

The First Clue Abroad

The opulent grandeur of the diplomat's apartment hits Miranda with a strange familiarity, though she has never set foot here before. Her eyes survey the crime scene, noting the austere elegance of polished marble floors under her shoes, absorbing the air thick with the faint scent of expensive cologne clinging to the air like an unresolved whisper. Each room echoes with the silent tale of an abruptly ended life, and she meticulously records the gruesome details of a precise execution in her notebook. Her scribbles almost drown in her mind's paranoia. The suspect's claimed sleepwalking feels like a mockery of her profession, tangled in a lineage of unyielding trauma that she wishes were merely myths of fiction.

Detective Reed's voice rises above the layers of Miranda's thoughts, his skepticism as palpable as the perspiration that clings to his brow. He circles the center of the room, his eyes narrowed, the faint lines of frustration etched deeply into his features. “Another sleepwalker, hmm? Someone's running a circus here and we don’t even have clowns to entertain with,” he states, the sarcasm dripping from each word, though rooted in a serious dread that prickles at his tension. Miranda listens absently, the familiarity of Reed's spectrum of disbelief nudging at a memory she can’t quite grasp, casting shadows that dance just at the periphery of her consciousness.

Her heart tightens as she uncovers ties linking this murder to the same shadowy sleep clinic she’s investigated back home. The slippery connection is as elusive as a whisper in a windstorm. Despite the heavy redactions, the fragmented records yield a courtship of catastrophic implications. The weight of potential obfuscation adds a new layer to Reed's alarm, his attempts to acquire comprehensive medical records thwarted at every corner. She senses frustration on the rise—the kind that fuels any good detective comprehension amid a forest obscured by fog.

“How can there be so much missing?” Reed's voice shudders with impotent rage. “It’s like someone’s got a handsaw and chopped out the truth, leaving us with knots and sawdust.”

She barely responds, too absorbed in decoding the miraculous nature of her déjà vu—a haunting melody born from forgotten sheets of notes she once knew by heart. Snatches of a past life rampant with programmed chaos flit past her vision, intermingling with present uncertainties that crawl under her skin. Her insides whirl with confusion and fear, a storm of doubt lashing at her mental barriers.

A cascade of incomprehensible recognition surges through her veins as her eyes drift over expensive art that gazes back at her, calling out from another time. Miranda stands rooted beneath a canvas depicting the ocean's fury, evoking a feeling she recalls with unsettling vividness. From its brine and chaos emerges a whisper of her own name, a name she owned and shed like Serpentskin. She's caught in a torrent of time—here, yet slipping incorporeal, spinning in the black hole of her resurrected memories.

Miranda’s knees almost buckle as she braces against the heavy doorframe, the room blurring into a kaleidoscope of remembrances and shadows. Doubt battles her clarity, merciless and primal, threatening the scaffolding of her carefully constructed defenses. Impressions of her forgotten past wage a silent war with every organ, echoing a truth only she can unravel. The diplomat's apartment breathes with an absence of resolution—just another piece in the puzzle demanding comprehension of what remains hidden in both her past and present.

The Redacted Files

Beneath the dim fluorescent glow, Miranda Carter navigates the winding corridors of Berlin's health records office. The shadows stretch long and lean against the institutional gray walls, echoing with the whispers of past transgressions. Her heart thrums a steady rhythm of urgency as she leads Detective Alex Reed into the depths of bureaucracy's iron grip, the allure of answers pulling them ever forward.

Miranda's mind is a maelstrom of determination and unease. The cold precision of her thoughts clashes with the murmurs of doubt, echoes of a time when her very identity hung in the balance. The memory of the sleep clinics, where control had been ripped from her hands, fuels her drive. Here, where secrets are entombed in file cabinets and digital vaults, freedom feels both elusive and cathartic.

When they reach the central records room, layers of security confront them—daunting but not insurmountable. Surveillance cameras cast sporadic glances, as if shrugging off responsibility, while security codes guard the information with bureaucratic ferocity. Miranda sets to work, her fingers dancing over keyboards, bypassing systems with deft assurance. Reed watches, his presence grounding her, though his silence reverberates with an unspoken desire for progress.

She combs through files, each scroll and click uncovering a sliver more of the obscured past. The victims' histories converge in disturbing similarities—their treatment paths eerily aligned. It's as if a puppeteer pulled the strings of their fates in synchrony. The weight of discovery rests heavy on her shoulders, driving her deeper into the twists of information.

Reed stirs behind her, his frustration palpable in the impatient shuffling of paper. "Is there no end to these redactions?" he mutters, a sharp edge to his voice. "It's like they're hiding something—or everything."

"Every thread we pull," she replies, not tearing her gaze from the screen, "it leads us to this fog. It's by design. Fragmented truths." Her conviction runs through her like a snare drum, each beaten pulse drawing her closer to that nebulous core where personal and professional strife perfectly collide.

"Do you think they knew?" Reed challenges softly, stepping closer, peering over her shoulder at the labyrinthine codes and names.

"I think they wanted us to reach this point and stumble," she admits, "but we're moving too fast for them." Her words are resolute, yet her mind questions whether speed will overcome the tidal wave of revelations that threaten to drown them.

Together, they weave through the data, whittling away at evasions that seem designed to push them back at every turn. As the computer hums in time to Miranda's rapid tapping, shadows from her past glance off the monitor, reflections of battles fought for identity and clarity. Each keystroke resounds with her refusal to be ensnared by history's grasp once more.

They press on, seeking tangible truths. Answers shimmer on the horizon, elusive yet ever closer, tantalizing in their promise of resolution. As they leave the office, the night air bites at their skin, invigorating in its chill. Moonlight bathes the street in an ethereal glow, casting long silhouettes that chase their steps, propelling them with the weight of shared determination.

Amid the silence of their exit, Miranda feels a connection —a burgeoning alliance, strengthened against the unseen force they both stand to defy. There is a storm brewing, both within her and beyond. The spectral remnants of old obligations mix with the hope of new dawns, whispering of a journey yet uncharted and a quest far from over.

Miranda's Night Terror

Miranda's eyes blur as they attempt to focus on the tangled pile of records spread out before her. The dim overhead light of the records office casts an unforgiving glare on the chaos, each document a taunting reminder of the labyrinthine truth she desperately seeks. As her vision clouds further, a sudden vertigo consumes her, and the world slips away, leaving her consciousness adrift in a sea of unlit memories.

Moments later, Miranda rouses to find herself sitting at a small table in a quiet Berlin café, the rich aroma of coffee enveloping the tranquil surroundings. Sunlight slants gently through the large windows, casting warm pools of illumination across the polished wooden floors. She struggles to reconcile the calm with the storm of confusion raging within her—how she managed to get here is a mystery tangled in the fog of her blackout.

The café around her thrums with polite conversations, a stark contrast to the turmoil exhausting her thoughts. Faces pass in a blur, brief flashes of curiosity hidden behind polite expressions. She knows this feeling too well; it's the sting of being judged through a lens fractured by unspoken truths. Her mind flits back to the days of Project Morpheus, the shadows of past missions clinging to her like an unwanted second skin.

The distant bell of a closing door draws Miranda's attention to Detective Reed, whose familiar presence approaches with hurried determination. His eyes hold a depth of concern, each wordless inquiry a reflection of the worried storm swirling within her. Doubt claws at Miranda's resolve, gnawing at the edges of her sanity, seeding the dark fear that she is losing control of her own mind.

"You okay?" Reed's voice is low, laden with unasked questions. He slides into the seat across from her, his gaze unwavering, intent on capturing whatever flickers of truth he can find in her eyes.

"Fine," Miranda lies, the word twisting in her voice like a tangled thread. "Just... trying to piece everything together."

A murmur of apprehension colors Reed's features, mismatched with the sunny morning beyond. "We need to stay focused, Miranda. These blackouts... they're getting worse."

Miranda sits rigid against the familiarity of his worry, memories surging unbidden as she fights to keep the tide of her past at bay. She relives the hours spent as a carefully engineered instrument in the hands of architects like The Warden, who twisted trust into a weapon, as sharp and precise as a scalpel. The remnants of her life veer dangerously close to erasure, coaxed by unseen forces yet to reveal themselves.

"There are threads," she whispers, more to herself than to Reed. "Threads connecting all of this... stretching right back to Morpheus."

Reed's fingers drum restlessly against the table, his unease mirrored in the caffeine-scented air. A stolen glance around the room brings to mind the circles of spectators in the amphitheater of her thoughts, marking the worry of those who witness without truly seeing. The pressure builds—not just from the implicit judgment of strangers, but from the weight of knowing that each step forward threatens to peel back layers of a life precariously balanced on a knife's edge.

Miranda holds the table's edge as if it might tether her to something more substantial than the swirling storm inside. A part of her yearns fiercely for clarity, an anchor in the tempest that her existence has become. She knows the puzzle pieces remain scattered, waiting for the precious moment of truth that might bind them together into a picture of betrayal wrapped in a conspiracy older than memory, and perhaps darker than she dares to imagine.

A Hidden Connection

In the cramped seclusion of the motel room, Miranda Carter sits hunched over the array of records sprawled on the narrow desk. The dim light casts a wavering halo around her as her eyes dart vigorously across the pages. It's here, buried under layers of coded bureaucracy, that a symbol repeatedly emerges, taunting her from the margins of grainy documents.

Her fingers trace the pattern—a stark symbol intertwined amid numbers and letters, each appearance a revelation. Her mind races, weaving fragments of memory with her knowledge of governmental operations. It's not just a pattern; it's a map, a code marking the Morpheus project files.

Beneath her composed facade, Miranda grapples with a sense of betrayal as the enormity of her past with Project Morpheus looms large. She recalls endless halls of sterile corridors, whispers of manipulation and control, and the chilling certainty that those tumultuous days haven't faded but linger in the seams of her present life. The systems she once trusted are intricately laced with manipulation, and a familiar paranoia coils around her thoughts like tendrils of smoke, threatening to smother her perceptions.

She realizes with growing dread that this symbol, this breadcrumb trail, signifies a carefully crafted chaos. Sleeper agents, unwitting and ever dormant, have the potential to unravel societal order with a single, strategic activation. The stakes are no longer confined to individual lives but stretch conspiratorially across borders, tugging at the integrity of governments, teetering on the brink of collapse.

Reed, resolute and determined, joins her, diving with equal fervor into decoding the enigma. His presence, solid and unwavering, offers a shared refuge of focus as they unearth further connections. His fingers move deftly over the keyboard, pulling up additional files, while Miranda articulates her deductions. Their collaboration, driven by a relentless push for transparency, starts piecing together a mosaic of governmental deceit.

They delve deeper into the digital seduction arrayed before them, uncovering layer upon layer of government machinations—each piece a cryptic hint towards a vault of secrets long protected. Among their collected wisdom rests the promise of understanding, but also the peril of facing a leviathan that never sleeps.

"Did you see this?" Miranda points at the screen, the coded display blinking threateningly back at them. "It's woven through everything. They're everywhere, and they're ready."

Reed nods, brow furrowed. "We've got to get in deeper. There has to be a way to blow this wide open."

She can hear the weight in his voice, the unspoken acknowledgment of the risk and the potential fallout. But there's no turning back, no evading the irresistible pull of the truth.

"Let's keep going. We've come this far," Miranda insists, the echo of her resolve filling the room.

Their work is methodical, stripping back the layers of encryption that veil the truth, like pulling away shadows from a hidden tableau. Each solved conundrum offers a peek into corridors of power where invisible hands orchestrate the dance of chaos. Their unity, Miranda realizes, is a bulwark against the isolation she feels creeping at the edges of her sanity.

As the last file closes, the room settles into silence, interrupted only by the occasional distant hum of Berlin's nightlife filtering through the paper-thin walls. Around them, the records lie dormant—the evidence of a conspiracy and the subtle promise of a world teetering on the brink. Miranda leans back, exhaustion competing with a quiet conviction; the pursuit is harrowing, but necessary. In the quiet, they both sense the palpable expectation of what's to come, knowing that they stand at the precipice of uncovering truths that could shape history.

The Silent Watcher

The night air in Berlin wraps around Miranda and Reed as they step into the darkness, the city's twinkling lights casting fragmented glimmers across the cobblestone streets. A chill whispers against Miranda's skin, weaving an unsettling narrative of shadows playing upon her senses. Each footfall reverberates against the quiet, echoing a cacophony of unease within her mind. They walk briskly, a shared silence enveloping them, yet there's no escaping the sensation of eyes upon their backs, watching, waiting.

Miranda can't shake the feeling that the city itself is holding its breath, poised for some unseen specter to emerge and claim the tranquility. There's a latent energy threading through the cool night air, alerting her to the presence lurking just out of sight. With every step, her tension mounts—an insidious pull she can't fault herself for feeling. Though they are supposedly alone, instincts warn her that they are subjects in someone else's clandestine theater.

They navigate through the dim alleyways, a silent choreography in tandem with their surroundings, attuned to the peculiarities of their environment. A moment passes, drawing her attention to a subtle shift in the atmosphere—a shadow sliding effortlessly behind. Her instincts scream; they are being pursued, not by the wavering lamplight, but by a watchful predator anchored to stealth and intent.

"This doesn't feel right," Miranda murmurs, acknowledging the palpable tension that now drapes over their camaraderie. The quiet undertones betray an intimacy forged under duress, where trust is both their ally and adversary.

"You're certain?" Reed questions, his voice a study of practiced composure now tinged with concern.

"It's as if the city is leading us somewhere we shouldn't be," she replies enigmatically, her mind caught in the trap of thoughts spiraling back to Project Morpheus, to pieces of a sinister puzzle just within reach, yet veiled in shadow.

They turn a corner, veering into another lane lined by dormant shops with shuttered windows, the narrative of exchanged glances speaking volumes to their awareness of each other's presence. The silence resumes, intercut only by the distant symphony of Berlin's nightlife, an auditory tapestry weaving its own stories in the spaces between.

Meanwhile, a silhouette moves with feline discretion, the tracker's gaze never wavering from its quarry. The streets become a serpentine labyrinth, wrapping around Miranda and Reed like an unfolding enigma. The observer lingers within a cloak of urban anonymity, cascading tendrils of darkness quilting their movements. A chilling anticipation spikes the night air, informing this silent witness that their quarry is oblivious to the invisible signals exchanged within the shadows.

The silhouette pauses, fingers quickly tapping a message into a device, the keystrokes virtually inaudible against the gentle breeze. Swift as the night is opaque, the communiqué finds its digital channel, whispered to a clandestine recipient: The Warden. Calculations born of a voiceless network deliver the knowledge: Miranda's investigation unfolds with acute alacrity.

"There's little comfort in obscurity," Miranda breathes, feeling Reed's presence beside her solid and reassuring, yet her thoughts stray into abstraction, into the veiled mechanics of the world they tread.

His response is measured, an exhalation that carries both solidarity and the subtle understanding binding them to a shared mission. "It's the knowledge that we're choosing the unknown," Reed offers, kindling a flicker of resilience.

Miranda nods, the cityscape tethering her focus to temporal paths converging beneath unseen layers. As they continue through Berlin's night, harmony and discord envelop their steps—an unending prelude to unknown chapters.

Above them, the vast night stretches endlessly, the stars punctuating the heavens in a constellation of whispered promises and silent betrayals. The observer halts, absorbing the tension as it diffuses into Berlin's night. Forces align and diverge in an omnipresent struggle between seen and unseen. With a practiced turn, the silhouette slips into the numinous margins of alleys, melding seamlessly into the city that knows just when to hold its secrets and when to let them linger.

Escaping the optics of mortal intrigue, Miranda and Reed journey onward, unknowing architects of fates interwoven with clandestine threads, in a city poised to witness what lies beyond the veil.

CHAPTER 3

THE LAB IN UKRAINE

The Underground Facility

In the waning dusk of Kyiv, an oppressive silence blankets the entrance to the underground facility. Rust-streaked walls and overgrown weeds paint a vivid image of abandonment, whispering ghostly tales of what once transpired within. Miranda Carter stands at the forefront, her pulse a quiet drumbeat in the solemn air. Beside her, Detective Alex Reed shifts his weight, the shuffling of his feet the only sound in the gathering gloom.

The door barring their way is marked with faded warnings, "Authorized Personnel Only," words barely visible through layers of grime. Miranda and Reed work in unison, using the tools they'd brought to tease open its rusty lock, the metallic groan of resistance eventually surrendering to their determination. They step into what feels like another world—a corridor steeped in darkness, cloaked with decades of dust and forgotten equipment.

The facility extends before them like a passageway into her own nightmares. Dim, foreboding lights flicker above, casting long, eerie shadows that dance across peeling paint and deserted desks. Miranda's breath comes shallow and sharp, every step through the hallway a symphony of creaks and echoes. In the recess of her mind, she knows this place's legacy—the ghosts of Project Morpheus, where next-level manipulations were tested and twisted beyond ethical reason.

As they move deeper, flicking through the pages of faded documents scattered haphazardly across forgotten desks, Miranda feels a strange pull, an unsettling familiarity embedding itself in her consciousness. Her eyes skim over personnel rosters and old clinic notes, a shiver running through her at the sight of her own name, bold and stark, penned as both subject and observer of callous experimentation.

The room seems to tilt, flattening against the weight of her discovery. Time pauses, every heartbeat hammering against her ribs as the realization anchors her. Her name, indelible among lists of victims and pawns, sets the fabric of her reality unraveling. The specter of Project Morpheus is more than a shadowy memory; it's a blood-stained fingerprint upon her very identity.

"Could it really be this bad?" Miranda murmurs, eyes wide, hands gripped tightly around the fragile edges of the file. Her voice barely trembles above a whisper, a distant call echoing through the dimness.

Reed takes a step closer, his expression shrouded in semi-darkness, offering only his presence. There's a moment's pause, where the enormity of their task grins back at them.

"We always knew this place would hold secrets," Reed replies, his tone attempting reassurance but weighted under the same grim revelation. "But finding yourself a part of them... Miranda, are you okay?"

Her fingers brush the edges of the brittle paper, as if by touch she could somehow comprehend the breadth of what had been done, what had taken root in the far corners of her mind. "I used to think the past was something you just lived through. It was done. But this, finding this..." Her breath hitches, the words tangled between disbelief and fear, "It means I've been a player and a pawn."

Reed nods, an unspoken understanding forming in the shared silence. He glances toward the corridor leading deeper into the decrepit shrine of Morpheus, the uncertainty in his eyes mirrored in hers. "Whatever happened here, we'll uncover it together. And we'll stop them. You aren't what they made you."

Miranda looks up, the shadows from overhead blurred with a resolve that's beginning to coalesce. The dusty records feel treacherously alive in her grip, more than echoes of bygone days—they're remnants of a past that had never let her go. "I hope you're right," she whispers.

She raises her gaze, torn between the broken office remains and the reality of the revelations she holds. As heavily as the shadow of Project Morpheus looms, the deeper truth lies not with the documents she clutched, but within her memories—vivid, raw, and irrepressibly significant to whom she is becoming.

The Patient Files

The rain sends tiny ripples through the puddles on the cobblestone street as Miranda and Reed approach the café, a quaint haven amidst the bustling decay of Kyiv. Inside, the world becomes muted, the scent of fresh coffee mingling with an undercurrent of tension. Dmitri Volkov sits at a secluded corner table, his gaze flitting to the window and back, like a sentry scanning for shadows. His eyes, creased with years of secrets and regrets, lock onto Miranda and Reed as they slide into seats across from him.

Dmitri's heart feels like a leaden weight within his chest, burdened by the memories of friends lost to the grim machinations of Project Morpheus. The program had its roots planted deep in the soil of governmental ambition, a psychological weapon designed to manipulate and control, its talons reaching across oceans, embedding sleeper agents in the veins of critical systems worldwide. Where Dmitri once saw order in the world, now stood paranoia—a specter that haunted him relentlessly, a constant whisper that even his shadow could not be trusted.

He feels the familiar guilt gnawing at him, a creature of his own making. For years, he had been the architect of some of those shadows, an actionable piece in Morpheus's puzzle before understanding the full extent of its implications. Each name on the project's ledger was a name he could have saved, each lost life a ghost in his own haunted hall. When he speaks, it's with an urgency clipped by fear—a need to shield these two from the dark fringe of his past.

"Glad you made it," Dmitri begins, his voice threaded with a rough edge. "Morpheus is a hydra, with reach deeper than just Ukraine or even America. We're talking global. Agents in government, finance, communication—you name it. They're embedded deep, ready to awaken."

Reed nods slowly, his eyes hardening as he absorbs the gravity of the situation. Miranda leans in slightly, aware of Dmitri's darting glances towards the café's other patrons, all while deciphering his every nuance. But Dmitri's mind whirls with the knowledge that at any moment, someone might watch, someone might suspect —an unease borne of too many years amid the unseen warfare of espionage.

"What's your next step?" Reed asks, attempting to steer the conversation back to strategy.

Dmitri leans forward, lowering his voice to a gravelly whisper. "You need to leave Ukraine. Yesterday, if possible. It's not just the agents you need to worry about, it's the specter of Morpheus lurking around every corner. This investigation is lighting up radars. You're being watched—and that's just the start."

His fingers tap a silent rhythm on the table, the remnants of a habitual tic. He recalls the hushed arguments in clandestine backrooms, colleagues who had once thrived in duty-bound loyalty, now discovered as either vanished or converted by the very cause he once championed. Dmitri fights down a shudder, feeling a bitter edge of desperation seep into his words.

"You have to understand," Dmitri continues, urgency bleeding through his tone. "They're watching and waiting for you to slip. If you linger too long, getting out becomes more than just difficult—it becomes impossible."

Miranda's gaze is steady, reflecting both determination and the shadow of dawning dread. Decisions scratch at the surface of her composure, weighing the risks cumulatively against the fragmentary truth they clutch like lifelines.

Dmitri watches her, grappling with a need to atone for mistakes past. "The longer this goes on, the longer you stay, the more dangerous this becomes for all of us."

Around them, the café churns with innocuous conversation, patrons oblivious to the undercurrents of danger that ripple between Dmitri, Miranda, and Reed. Dmitri checks the time and takes a last sip of the cooling beverage, a grounding ritual, stark against the persistent rise of dread.

His voice hoarsens with a plea rounded by unspoken terror. "Move quickly—and be careful." He surveys the café, the world beyond it closing tighter. "They're closer than you think."

With a final, tense nod, Dmitri returns to scanning the room, his caution an overture, a protective cloak for the warnings now spun into thc air likc unsteady threads.

The Sniper's Ambush

Reed pushes the café door open, the jingle of the bell overhead nearly drowned out by the rush of the bustling Kyiv street. He steps into the twilight, Miranda on his heels, when the world snaps into sharp focus—crack! The sniper's bullet slices through the air, a sinister whisper against the city's evening symphony. Instinct pulls them low as they dive for cover, rolling behind the first parked cars they encounter.

The metallic taste of adrenaline clogs Reed's senses. He's back in training, every nerve electrified, his field of view distilled to a narrow tunnel of survival. His breath comes fast as he scans the rooftops. There—you skulking predator, concealed against the fading light. The glint of a scope reflects momentarily, pinpointing the hunter high above.

All while covering Miranda with one arm, he makes his calculations. The sniper has the advantage, holding higher ground and the element of surprise, but Reed has unpredictability. In a panicked city where shadows move like liquid, he has learned the importance of becoming one with chaos.

"Miranda," he breathes, the tone a hushed command, "on my mark, we move." He's relying on her instincts, honed by Morpheus—a program deepened in brutality yet sharpened by necessity. Her nod, brief and almost imperceptible, is all the confirmation he needs. She's a puzzle to him, pieces fractured and scattered yet bound together by an indomitable will. That same will has been her shield, buoying her through every twist and revelation.

The sniper is less patient than expected; another shot clangs off metal, ricocheting into the night. Reed might have marveled at the sniper's steady focus, had the situation not been laced with mortal peril. He's out of time.

"Now!" Reed yells, and they're sprinting—two stark silhouettes against the cobbled streets, feet pounding with a rapid urgency. He leads them, instinctively taking the longer route toward the alley, shoulders brushing against walls, the path narrowing with each desperate step. Each corner they turn holds potential salvation or doom, and Reed feels the weight of this leaden decision on his heart.

As they clear the last stretch, he steels himself and takes a glance over his shoulder. The sniper's position hasn't wavered—still an eagle-eyed specter in the city's dusk. His tactical mind runs through options—a counteroffensive, an attempt at diplomacy, any stratagem to shield their mission from this unseen foe. But as plans fragment and slip through his grasp, the alley looms close, beckoning escape.

Before the alley, Reed snatches a final silent agreement with Miranda—a glance shaded with the gravity of life and death. It vibrates with unspoken certainty: retreat, survive, continue the struggle. His instincts roar with urgency; her fractured past has interwoven with his, crafting ephemeral bonds solidified only by shared survival.

In the echoing pulse of their collective escape, something congeals within him—perhaps hope tending to its ember, daring to flicker benevolently against the relentless backdrop of darkness they face. As the alley folds around them, swallowing them into its murky embrace, survival remains paramount. For now, the strike team of their singular unity, promises more than the bleakness of what hunts them.

Miranda reaches for calm amid chaos, the structured focus lending her buoyancy as she threads herself into their thumping retreat. The sniper's specter fades with every step, retreating into the confines of a distant threat they narrowly eluded. As the shadows deepen, mystery and memory entwine in her mind, weaving a tapestry marked not by gentle hues but by fear and ambiguous recollection. The cloak of her past theorem calls upon her, borrowed from the recesses of what is forgotten yet not laid to rest.

A Shadowy Informant

Adrenaline propels Miranda through the narrow alleys of Kyiv, her heart echoing in time with their footfalls on the cobblestones. Her surroundings blur into hurried shadows, yet flashes of a dim, clinical room—a place tinged with the sterile smell of antiseptic—begin to overlay the present chaos. Cold metal against skin, the relentless hum of fluorescent lights, the distant murmur of voices she can't quite place.

These visions crash over her, each wave pulling her further into memories she fights to keep submerged. Every stride through the winding streets unlocks another fragment—a kaleidoscope of confusion and desperation binding her mind. Tear across scalpels, numbers gravely recited, clinical detachment by robed figures with obscured faces. A sensation rises, curling through her like smoke: part revelation, part horror. The experiments of Project Morpheus had not only altered her—they had embedded shadows of themselves deep within.

"Miranda, stay with me!" Reed's voice cuts through, his hand a steady anchor against the tide of her unraveling past. His voice reminds her of the mission, of Tehran, of the need to reorient reality against the threatening maze of her thoughts.

But the memories persist. Faces blur past—patients like her in ghostly hospital gowns, eyes vacant yet pleading. She grasps their pain and knows with a harrowing certainty that their fates, bounded by invisible shackles, are interwoven with hers. Questions hammer at the facade of her current identity. Who was she really, if simply being a part of Morpheus made her a ghost in her own life?

"What's happening?" Reed's urgency morphs into something akin to fear, helmeted in pragmatic concern. She stumbles, vision again flickering to the monochrome greys of the lab, where thick files brandish her name against the void. She's there—caught in an endless loop between past and present, a prisoner of two times. Whose images haunt her dreams? Why are they stained with the echo of her own first screams?

The world narrows. Her pulse syncs with the tick of a distant clock—each beat a taunting whisper: You are part of this. Remember. Unearth the truth you dread.

He catches her as she falters, guiding her forward through the dankness of the alley, through the clutches of memory's returning embrace. "Miranda..." It's a plea now, a grounding force.

Suddenly, shards of lucidity pierce her haze. She gasps, pulling air deep into her chest, banishing apparitions with each exhale. The vision solidifies as she braces against the damp brick: rows of hospital beds, monitors casting sterile blue light, the sterile efficiency of it all drowning her with its familiarity. This is it—the heart of her entrapment.

"Keep moving!" The urgency in Reed's voice knits the seam of her reality, pulling her back from the precipice.

Miranda steadies herself, forehead pressed against the cold stone, eyes closing momentarily as clarity resurfaces. Who she is—who she might have been—melts beneath the unwavering necessity to survive, to unravel Morpheus's tangled web. Yet, as they flee further into the Kyiv shadows, she acknowledges the truth. This knowledge—these memories—are hers, and they demand reckoning.

As they disappear into the safety of another narrow, twisting lane, Reed's hand at her elbow, a certainty creeps through the fray: Everything about who she once knew herself to be is forever altered. Yet, within this chaos, she discovers a resolve. Alongside Reed's fierce determination, she clutches onto the splintered truth she's unearthed. She must follow these compass points, wherever they may lead, if she is to find the reality of her life beyond Morpheus's reach.

The Lost Memories and The Next Target

The safe house stands on the outskirts of Kyiv, a forgotten relic wrapped in the gauze of urban decay. Darkness settles like a shroud over its peeling walls and creaking floorboards, casting eerie shadows that flicker with each gust of wind. Inside, the place feels like a cocoon spun from silence and secrecy, sheltering secrets so precarious they might fracture at the slightest disturbance. But here, under the veil of night, Miranda and Reed regroup, their breaths mingling with the still air, heavy with the staleness of a refuge both temporary and unnervingly familiar.

Miranda sits at a scarred wooden table, papers strewn before her like the jigsaw pieces of an unspeakably complex puzzle. Her hands tremble slightly as she reaches for a crumbling dossier, eyes scanning the pages that hold their future entwined with the horrid specters of their past. Her mind drifts momentarily, the oppressive weight of uncertainty pressing down on her chest, reminding her of the boundaries she can neither wholly embrace nor escape. She clings desperately to the notion of carving out a life untainted by Morpheus, yet fears that true liberation might be as illusory as the shadows that dance across the room.

Reed settles opposite, eyes alert yet rimmed with fatigue, as if the very tendrils of Project Morpheus have wound themselves within his soul, threatening to unravel him at any second. "Tehran," he says, breaking the silence as his finger taps on one of the papers. "We're looking at sleeper agents ready to ignite political chaos. It's a matter of when, not if."

Miranda nods, her focus trained on the coded fragments of information lodged like time-bombs throughout the documents. "The message points to an assassination," she murmurs, her voice barely above a whisper, laden with a mixture of dread and resolve.

"Can we stop it in time?" Reed's question punctuates the air, wavering between hope and hopelessness.

Without lifting her gaze, Miranda sets to work decoding. A pattern emerges, an intricate dance of symbols and numbers, aligning to reveal Tehran as the next target in a cruel game orchestrated by invisible hands. Her stomach churns at the realization of another city poised on the brink, lives balanced precariously on the slumber of agents who are anything but asleep. She battles the impulse to let panic overwhelm her, forces herself to focus, to breathe.

Reed's voice cuts through her swirling thoughts. "If we head straight there, we might have enough time to figure out their plan and act." His words are a lifeline, tethering her to the task at hand, providing a blueprint amid the chaos.

"They'll expect you to intervene, Reed," she says, pushing through the fog of her own uncertainty. She concentrates on his familiar profile, hoping for some sign of his resilience.

"We can't think of that now. What's important is preventing what's about to come," he assures her.

Their decision is unspoken but solidified in shared determination. Reed begins packing the documents with meticulous care, knowing each word, each number, is a thread in the fragile tapestry they must weave to safeguard lives. Meanwhile, Miranda leverages their scant resources to send out an encrypted message, her fingers dancing across the device, signaling their impending arrival to a trusted contact in Tehran. The urgency of their mission hangs like a noose in the small room, the cold bite of inevitability chilling her resolve.

There, amidst the ghosts of past wrongs and the specter of future uncertainty, Miranda steels herself for the next chapter of their journey. Both a fugitive and a seeker, she moves with the inevitability of someone who understands that escaping the past is a task as Herculean as it is essential. The shadows recede ever so slightly, yielding to a glimmer of dawn over the horizon, beckoning her to step forth into the unknown once more.

CHAPTER 4

THE CHASE IN TEHRAN

Veils of Betrayal in Tehran

Daylight pours over the Tehran marketplace, where vibrant colors and a tapestry of sounds weave a lively atmosphere. The air is thick with the blend of spices and freshly baked bread, mingling with the hum of merchants and customers haggling over prices. Amidst this cacophony, Miranda Carter feels a squeeze of anxiety in her chest, her senses stretching to the limit as she navigates through the throng alongside Reed.

Their target is Farid Mansour—a connection layered with the promise of revealing grim truths about sleeper agents like the ones they now stalk. Miranda tunes into the cadence of the market, where faces blur into one another. Each unfamiliar glance nettles her instincts; she is acutely aware that even minor gestures could whisper volumes about hidden intentions.

The din around them stands in stark contrast to the quiet paranoia simmering in Miranda's mind—the awareness that amidst this seemingly commonplace gathering, danger coexists with normalcy. A flash of realization hits her as she observes families, friends, and vendors oblivious to the covert horrors lurking in Tehran. Beyond the vibrant bazaar façades lies a tangled web of programming and deceit, bearing the fingerprints of

Project Morpheus. It's a world where silent terrors ripple under the surface, leaving society to grapple with a fragile sense of trust toward intelligence operations.

Miranda's phone vibrates abruptly, stirring her from her ruminations. Farid provides swift instructions, guiding them toward a more secluded venue for their exchange. Miranda remains vigilant, consciousness colored by the weight of decisions past and the indelible marks of her former involvement in Morpheus. Despite standing amidst bustling life, the gulf between what she was and who she might be stretches vast and intimidating.

Navigating the market is like weaving through a living tapestry, where stalls boast fruits with hues as vivid as the Persian tales spun by ancestors under these ancient skies. Yet beneath its energy, a pall of clandestine anxiety persists. Miranda and Reed push past alleys narrow and dimly lit until they reach the spot—a shadowed enclave removed from the crowd.

Farid is there. His presence feels substantial but brief, holding the scent of revelations yet untold. Even as their conversation begins, tension vibrates in the air like a wire pulled at both ends. Words barely emerge before chaos claims the calm—a crescendo of violence eats away at the scene's peace when shots ring out, cleaving through their assembly.

Miranda reacts with instinctual precision, launching into cover as gunfire ricochets off the alley walls. She finds herself alongside Reed, adrenaline a swift current, eyes meeting his in that suspended moment when uncertainty brushes fingertips with purpose. In this shared gaze, they acknowledge a singular truth: action is their only anchor in this storm. Together, they brace against the eruption of chaos, each parsing thought translating into calculated, silent resolve.

Fractured Refuge

Amidst the fading echoes of gunfire, Miranda and Reed sprint through the winding alleyways of Tehran, their footfalls resonating against the stone walls. The rhythm of their rushing hearts matches the chaotic drum of the distant market, where life continues to pulse despite the violence that just erupted. Miranda clutches her side, her breath ragged as she processes the narrow escape from death's grasp, each step reminding her of the fragile line between life and oblivion.

The haze of fear dissipates as they find refuge in the belly of an abandoned building. Silence swallows them whole, the once piercing symphony of city life reduced to a muted whisper. The air here is stagnant, each inhalation tinged with mildew and decay, starkly opposing the vibrant chaos they fled. Leaning against the cold surface of the crumbling plaster, Miranda's pulse finally begins to slow, the cold seeping into her bones even as it fails to quiet her mind.

Confinement gives way to contemplation, a space where Miranda could unravel the threads of moments past. Her thoughts swirl in an untenable dance—worries about the agents they escaped, doubts about Mansour's fatal end, fears of what lies ahead. Yet her mind refuses to dwell on any single point for long, unwilling to allow the full weight of reality to settle. As daylight wavers, tinges of a steely gray dusk descend, not enough to dispel the gathering shadows within her mind.

Then, a cold shiver runs through her. A sudden pang of disorientation roots her to the spot, her consciousness flickering like a candle battling against an unseen draft. The steady sanctuary within her vanishes in an instant, plunging her into an abyss where shadows of memories snag her like thorns—real and unreal, as indistinguishable as mist.

A breath later, Miranda is back in the tangible world, the metallic tang of copper saturating the air. Her fingers curl around the hilt of a blood-stained knife, its surface sticky with still-warm life's blood, an accusing testament to deeds she cannot recall. Nausea churns through her, a rising tempest that crashes hard against her insides, threatening to break through her strained composure. Her sight swims, anchored only by the cold reality of weapon and wound, though both are strangers to her memory.

Broken gasps fill the empty space, the weight of the evidence dragging her down with inexorable force—each crimson drop a point on a map she cannot recall navigating. Miranda's vision narrows, her grip on reality as precarious as the knife she wields. Dread coils tight, whispering doubts she dares not entertain, whispering that she, not the world she battles, is her own enemy.

Reed stands nearby, a solid presence in the encroaching void, his expression unreadable to her but a lifeline all the same. As the spectral hands of paranoia tug at her, Miranda finds herself reaching for him, seeking refuge despite the chasm of uncertainty yawning wide before her. She anchors herself to his form, trembling fingers clinging to the fabric of his coat as if it can keep her anchored in the real, the present.

Surrounded by the encroaching shadows, her reflection flickers in the dim periphery—scattered pieces held together by will alone. The dichotomy leaves her spinning, balance lost between the memory of something unremembered and the comfort of Reed's reassuring steadiness. She longs to voice her fears, to transform doubt into clarity, but the words remain knotted, refusing passage from her throat.

An alley becomes a sanctuary, though it offers no solace. Here, surrounded by silence and stone, Miranda realizes that within the wall's confines she must reconcile remnants of her buried past—the truth weaved within her blackouts and the fate waiting to unfurl. Yet for now, she finds strength in Reed's presence, for in his grounded assurance, she senses the path forward. Reluctantly, she releases the knife, its clatter against the floor a distant sound drowned in her mind's roar. All she knows is that beneath the shadows lies an answer she must unravel, and somehow, she will find it.

Miranda's Blackout Returns

Reed stares into the dim light filtering through the cracked windows, his gaze shifting across the barren room, alert and probing. Shadows stretch across the floor, each creak of the building settling tugging at his nerves. Miranda attempts to steady her breath, each inhale heavy with the adrenaline still coursing through her veins. Her mind feels fragmented, each piece refusing to settle back into a coherent whole.

She presses her back against the cool, gritty wall, trying to shut out the disquieting blur of thoughts and memories that refuse to align. Flashes of the ambush flare behind her eyes: Farid's shocked expression, the sudden crack of gunfire, the desperate scramble for safety. They merge seamlessly into other memories—training sessions, her mentor's dispassionate critiques, missions undertaken without question—all muddy the waters of her mind. She couldn't help but wonder if the person she was trained to be overrides who she believes she is now. She yearns for detachment from that past, yet its shadow lingers, heavy and suffocating.

A sharp metallic beep punctures the silence. Miranda flinches, her pulse quickening as she fumbles for her phone. The screen glows with an ominous message: "You were never supposed to wake up." The cold, clinical words seem cruelly intimate, pricking at her carefully constructed defenses. These words, terse yet loaded, clutch at the edges of her certainty, mocking the freedom she so desperately desires.

Reed peers over her shoulder, his breathing quickening as he reads the message. Panic flashes in his eyes, reminding Miranda of the feral instincts that kept them both alive until now.

"We have to go," he insists, urgency threading his tone, itself a demand as much as a plea. "It's not safe. They could be tracking your phone. We need to put distance between us and them."

"I—I didn't even remember..." Miranda stammers, struggling against the avalanche of fear threatening to envelop her. Her voice falters, caught between disbelief and disquiet. Her identity feels fragile, grasped in the grip of forces she can barely understand, let alone control.

Reed remains firm, pushing aside any debate. "We don't have time to analyze. They'll be closing in. We need to move!"

Nodding, Miranda tosses her phone to the floor, a small act of defiance that punctuates her decision to sever links to whoever might be pulling their strings. The phone clatters away, taking a part of her uncertainty with it, even as the oppressive weight of The Warden's machinations feels more deeply embedded within her psyche.

A sense of resignation lingers. "I can't keep doing this... fighting shadows," she admits softly, more to herself than Reed, her voice tinged with a vulnerability she rarely exposes.

"We go forward," Reed replies with steadfast conviction. "We figure this out and stop The Warden for good. We have each other."

Miranda grips the edge of his arm, drawing strength from his certainty. In his eyes, she finds a reflection of determination she once held dear. With a last glance at what she left behind—the scornful message and shattered phone—they turn. As they step into the encroaching darkness beyond the building, their resolve knots together, binding them with a shared purpose, however uncertain their path may be.

Nightfall Pursuit

Emerging from the building, Miranda and Reed step into the night, the air thick with the sizzle of distant traffic and the pungent aroma of street vendors hastily packing up their stalls. Their senses sharpen, eyes flicking from shadow to shadow as they weave through the labyrinthine streets of Tehran. Each echoing footstep on the cobblestones sounds like mistimed drumbeats threatening to betray their position.

Miranda glances at Reed, a silent understanding passing between them—a mutual reliance forged in darkness and danger. Their bond has grown unexpectedly strong. Not by choice, but necessity, solidified with each close call and shared whispered strategy. Her life, once guided by logic and the cold comfort of data, now drifts through uncertainty like a ship at night, Reed her only anchor.

A sudden realization grips her heart with icy fingers—armed agents are closing in. The edges of their existence threaten to blur into indistinct silhouettes against the night sky. She motions to Reed, and they slip into a narrow, shadowed alleyway, the darkness swallowing their figures whole. Footsteps draw near, a rhythmic chase growing faster, louder, driving their every motion.

Her mind races alongside her feet. Miranda's past experiences—the churning chaos of life and death, the algorithmic precision with which missions were executed against unsuspecting targets—aloft the high stakes of espionage, flit through her consciousness. Her survival once hinged on these skills, and now, they are all she can depend on. For in this world, the line between agent and assignment blurs amidst blood and betrayal.

Yet here she is, guided not by orders, but by her will to escape, to unravel the truth that clings to each shadowy corner of her past. Each alley leads them closer to safety, each corner turned a potential salvation or trap. Her breath comes in shallow gasps but she presses on, driven by persistence instead of fear.

From behind, the relentless chorus of boots on pavement sends adrenaline surging anew. Instinct propels them forward, the cityscape a fragmented blur of neon lights and stone facades, weaving their way through the chaotic tapestry of Tehran. She and Reed, partners of circumstance, hover between worlds—hunted and hunter, protector and protected.

Their mutual grasp on the city's layout, honed from hours of study, becomes their lifeline. With precise movements they slip away from their pursuers, the cacophony of hurried shouts fading into obscurity. The tension, though momentarily behind them, clings to their every step like sweat under the skin.

In the brief reprieve, they halt, breaths mingling in the chill of the night. The danger is a living presence around them, a reminder hidden in each nook and cranny of this ancient city. Miranda looks at Reed, taking in the set of his jaw, the determination etched into his features. Trust—a hesitant bond sealed by shared struggles—binds them stronger than any contract from their past lives might have allowed.

But even here, in transient safety, a question looms between them, echoed in the silent streets and stifled breaths: how long can they run before the shadows catch up?

Shadows of Morpheus

Inside the cramped storage unit on the fringes of Tehran, Reed paces back and forth, the weight of the night's events heavy on his shoulders. The faint, persistent hum from the single bulb swings above as if echoing the turmoil in his mind. With each step on the cold concrete, he battles to keep his thoughts anchored, knowing Miranda needs him sharp for what lies ahead.

The very fabric of trust, so integral to his work as an investigator, feels threadbare against the backdrop of the manipulation orchestrated by Project Morpheus. Sleeper agents, scattered across continents, move like ghosts within organizations, their true purpose hidden even from themselves. Reed sees the insidious reach of Morpheus like an intricate map etched across the world, each line a tether to an unsuspecting soul. He imagines a web extending, threads of deception coiling around the hearts of governments and agencies alike, obscuring truth with practiced shadows.

Miranda's voice cuts through the silence and grounds him. "We have to get to Switzerland."

Reed nods, resting his back against a stack of wooden crates. "It's our best shot. Finding leads on Project Morpheus might just give us the leverage we need." His voice is steady, but beneath it, a current of urgency churns, pulling at the edges of control.

"We have to move before they seal us off," she insists, her words urging action, fanning any lingering hesitation.

As he scours through their limited assets, a grim acknowledgment surfaces: his own life twisted by the same sinister forces they now chase. Every revelation serves not as a key to understanding, but as a reminder of how entangled they have become. Did he act of his own free will, or was he merely following invisible strings he couldn't see until now? Doubt gnaws at him, leaving a raw wound exposed to the night air.

"Got something," Reed announces, pulling out a set of forged identities from a frayed folder. A cautious hope laces his tone. "Passports. They're solid enough to get us out of here."

"Good." Miranda returns his look with determination. For her, it's a necessity, a step forward into the proverbial lion's den where answers might await, wrapped in layers of danger.

He allows a brief smile, but inwardly, his thoughts spiral. What if Morpheus wasn't just an external project but a reflection of the worst humanity had crafted from itself? If every person harbored a fragment of that darkness, how could they ever be sure of themselves?

Handing over the passports, his fingers brush against hers, a fleeting contact that sparks a moment of clarity. "Let's focus on what needs to be done," he says, more to himself than to her, a mantra to quell the chaos within.

They pack hurriedly, adrenaline sharpening their senses to the muted metallic clangs and creaks that surround them. As night wraps its chilling embrace tighter, their hurried movements signal far more than just preparation for escape; it's an unspoken agreement to keep the horrors at bay, to oppose the uncertainty with the only things they can: action and resolve.

"We'll make it," Miranda urges, more to fortify herself than to reassure him. Her resolve is a balm to Reed's wavering spirit.

“Yes, we will.” He meets her gaze directly, letting the purpose they share illuminate a path through shadows.

The night presses in, the air dense with the stories of countless others who might have stood where they now do—defying the tyranny of unseen masters. Reed takes a deep breath, clinging to the belief that reclaiming his reality is within reach; a hope that perhaps amidst the web of Morpheus, the human spirit can still forge its own destiny.

CHAPTER 5

THE ESCAPE FROM TEHRAN

Rooftop Exodus

The air is thick with tension, an uninvited guest that has settled in with the stillness of the night. Miranda Carter stands by the window, the dim glow of the Tehran skyline framing her silhouette. It's been a long time since she last felt safe anywhere, and tonight is no exception. The image of her own face, drawn with weariness, stares back at her from the dark glass—both a comfort and a reminder of the precariousness of her existence.

A sudden crash breaches the room, shattering the fragile calm. The door swings open with the force of a hurricane, and Iranian intelligence agents spill into the space like an unstoppable tide. Instinct kicks in. Miranda and Reed exchange a swift, silent nod—no time for fear, only action. Together, they scramble, collecting what essentials they can. The room is a blur, the line between reality and chaos smudged by adrenaline and urgency.

Miranda's heart pounds in her chest, a relentless drumbeat driving her forward as the cold air grips them in its icy fist. She and Reed burst into the corridor, shadows dancing in the flickering light. The hotel, once a sanctuary, has turned into a labyrinth of danger. Floor by floor, they descend towards the emergency exit, every second a gamble in the fleeting game of survival. Desperation clings to them as tightly as their own skin.

The past, inescapable and oppressive, hovers on the fringes of Miranda's consciousness. It's all led to this, hasn't it? The web of lies and manipulations spun by the now-defunct Project Morpheus snares her once more. Genetic and psychological experimentation, they called it—the breeding ground for sleepers: unsuspecting pawns in a dangerous game. Those horrific experiments have stitched shadows into the fabric of her soul, and now the shadows approach again.

On the hotel's roof, they traverse the neighboring buildings, transforming the tenuous tightrope into a sanctuary from the prying eyes below. Beneath their feet, the city pulses with life, oblivious to the hunt unfolding in its midst. Ruins of the past shimmer into view as fleeting memories, fragments of the life she once knew, lived, and now just barely clings to.

They find their refuge in an alleyway, the entrance to an abandoned warehouse beckoning—a haven from the chaos. Miranda slumps against the cold embrace of a stone wall, taking a brief respite to recover. Reed stands beside her, steady amidst the chaos, always ready, always at her back. She draws a deep breath, her emotions, tumultuous and raw, barely contained beneath a thin veneer of calm.

Around them, the sirens wail—a symphony of urgency—and with each note, the world blurs a little more until it is just her, Reed, and the weight of everything that once was, everything that remains. The night is restless. The city is alive. And beneath the starlit canopy, hidden from view, Miranda and Reed cradle their fragile remnants of hope, aware that this battle, this war for their souls, is far from over.

Fractured Refuge

In the hushed darkness of the warehouse, beams of moonlight filter through cracked windows, casting eerie, distorted patterns on the cold concrete floor. Miranda huddles in the shadows with Reed, their breath mingling with the dust motes adrift in the stagnant air. Each anxious beat of her heart is a reminder of where she is—a liminal space between danger and fleeting safety—and of who she might be. A wave of memories from faceless corridors in her mind rush back: sterile rooms, sterile people, and the chilling sensation of not knowing whether she walked them as herself or as a tool for others.

Project Morpheus, she recalls, as if whispering to herself. An insidious program breeding a web of shadowy control, a siren's call to untapped human potential twisted into something altogether monstrous. How many had there been like her, wandering the precipice of autonomy, swayed by sinister notes only they heard? She wonders if each footfall she had taken led her unwittingly closer to that veritable edge, where activation awaited like an unseen snare. Could she have unknowingly authored some horror, penned dark chapters in a story she could not remember?

"You're quiet," Reed murmurs, his voice a low rumble cutting through her reverie. She can sense his concern, see it manifest in the candle flicker of a glance in her direction. The question hangs between them, unuttered and heavy: How deep in this are you? She hesitates before speaking, the words fragile on her lips.

"I sometimes think... what if I'm just part of it all?" Her voice trembles like the warehouse's roofing. "What if I did things? Horrible things, and I just can't remember?" The fear is palpable, a constricting hand around her throat. She wonders aloud about the nocturnal blackouts, the lost time that steals her sense of self.

Reed shifts, leaning his shoulder against a rusting support beam, the hard lines of his profile softened by shadows. "Whatever happened back then, you're not that person now," he reassures her, grounding her with his presence. "You won't be alone in this."

She catches the earnest resolve in his words, yet her spirit remains untethered, haunted by echoes of an unseen past. Each memory that bubbles up is more turbulent than the last: the sterile halls of her past now corridors lined with faces—not victims of her actions, perhaps, or maybe precisely that—but echoes she yearns to reconcile. But even in remembering, the visage of accountability is faceless. Is she perpetrator or prey—or both in cruel collusion?

A sudden awareness draws her back to their precarious hideout. Somewhere beyond the cracked walls, the murmured cadence of Iranian agents flickers like candlelight chasing shadows. The words reach her ears in fragmented melodies, each phrase a revelation—the widespread omnipresence of Project Morpheus, the tendrils that stretch beyond imagining. Her heart skips a beat, a frightening reminder of the scale of what they confront.

The weight grows heavier, clinging stubbornly to her like a cloak, as if by bearing it alone she hopes to achieve atonement. Reed's steadfast eyes find hers once more, a fragile tether in tumult. "You're keeping it together, despite everything," he says softly, his tone a balm to restless thoughts, even if only for a moment.

Miranda gives a terse nod, leaning against the frigid embrace of the wall, the weight of her conflicted emotions pressing against her chest. This battle with her own mind seems endless, but Reed provides a glimmer of stability—a reminder that amidst the chaos, there's hope. The distant footsteps grow louder, a reminder to stay vigilant in the face of advancing darkness. Together, they brace for what is to come.

Mid-Air Rebellion

Miranda and Reed slip into the shadowed alley behind the bustling market, anxiety gnawing at the edges of their resolve like hungry wolves. They meet their contact, a smuggler whose eyes dart nervously over his shoulder. He leads them to a rusty van, assuring them of a discreet passage to the airport, the words tumbling from his lips in hurried whispers. Miranda senses the urgency pulsing beneath his calm facade like distant thunder.

Once at the airport, the clamor of bustling travelers and the orchestrated chaos of departure lounges envelops them. Miranda's heart pounds a relentless drumbeat as they maneuver through the crowded terminal, aware of the lurking possibilities of capture. She gravitates towards the shadows, her ears tuned to the whispers of paranoia that haunt her thoughts—echoes of the past where duty blurred with exploitation, where trust became as brittle as frost-coated leaves.

On-board the dimly lit cargo plane, a chill clings to the air as Miranda settles into a creaking seat, her gaze flitting between passengers. Her thoughts descend into labyrinths of memory, tangled roots from which she cannot disentangle herself. Each encounter with The Warden during Project Morpheus resurfaces—a dance of manipulation where she was led to question her own sovereignty. Those memories seep like ink into her consciousness, tinting her perception and gnawing at her resolve to remain herself.

The plane lurches, settling into the fragility of flight. Miranda's instincts stay razor-sharp despite exhaustion tugging at her edges. As the craft climbs, the metal confines of the fuselage begin to feel suffocating. Buried scars ache like distant echoes within her—a reminder of how expertly The Warden preyed upon her vulnerabilities. Her fear clenches, a serpent coiled around her heart, as she fights to retain control over her fractured self in the face of whispers that insist she could be more than she perceives.

Inside the cockpit, a man—calm, yet unsettlingly detached—catches her attention, a dormant danger awakening in the depths of his eyes. A ripple of awareness spreads through the cabin, twisting the atmosphere tight with anticipation. The man rises, his motions deliberate, and pilots instinctively recognize the disruptive force that has taken hold; a sleeper agent no longer shackled by sleep's safe embrace.

Pandemonium unfolds as the pilot lunges; Miranda moves instinctively, driven by a necessity older than rational thought. Reed battles quaking controls while Miranda combats this harbinger of chaos—each movement a testament to the resilience she fights to reclaim. Awareness of life's delicacy tightens its grip, and the plane trembles, caught between gravity and those clutching salvation with white-knuckled fervor.

Miranda's every motion is steeped in desperation. The echo of urgency drums within her as the struggle tightens around the little universe contained within the plane's structure—her, Reed, and a destabilized man. The fight becomes an allegory for what it means to wrest subtle autonomy from the tyranny of destiny molded through Project Morpheus' clandestine designs.

With each thrust and parry, Miranda digs into raw resolve, forcing a connection between body and mind that signifies resilience. She remembers the fleeting moments The Warden deemed her an obedient puppet, a relic from a darkened theater accustomed to playing roles dictated by others. But now, Miranda fights back—not just with sinew and rage, but with an unwillingness to succumb to the veil of shadows.

The resolution is neither ebb nor silence, but a single precious heartbeat beyond chaos. The hijacker slumps, his eyes flickering with an extinguished echo of command, leaving Miranda and Reed gasping in the aftermath. In the cavernous quiet, the opportunity to regain order settles like a gentle promise—a lull before another storm lurking on the horizon. They brace themselves against the tightening grip of uncertainty, a new determination solidifying within them.

Turbulent Whispers

The cargo plane shudders mid-flight, metal groaning under the strain as turbulence rocks its belly. In the dimly lit cabin, the air feels stifling, the kind that wraps around Miranda and Reed in an invisible grip. They exchange a wary glance, an unspoken understanding of the danger they've narrowly escaped.

Miranda's heart races, not only from the fight that had just ensued but from the weight of their circumstances. Her earpiece crackles to life, a sinister whisper cutting through the static—a voice she knows too well.

"You were never meant to wake up, Miranda." The Warden's chilling message sends a jolt through her. She grips the edge of her seat, fighting the urge to yank out the earpiece and smash it beneath her boot.

His awareness of their every move, his unseen influence —a reminder of her days under Project Morpheus's thumb. Sessions meant to 'enhance' her potential, they called it, glazed with promises of control and power. But those promises were marred by glimpses of something darker—an unseen puppet master pulling strings, shaping destinies not their own. The echoes from those days reverberate with each recorded heartbeat, each whispered threat from The Warden, anchoring fear deep in her bones.

Miranda closes her eyes, trying to steady her breath as memories claw their way to the surface—the flash of white coats in sterile rooms, the needle's prick and the intoxicating fog of sedation. It had all been a façade, a charade that hid desires far more sinister than she had once allowed herself to believe. Every decision, every controlled moment, a strand in a web of manipulation designed to curb autonomy, not amplify it.

"Reed," she calls out, her voice barely rising above the drone of the engines. He turns, eyes heavy with the fatigue of their endless escapade. "The Warden knows. He's—" The words stick in her throat, as if saying them aloud solidifies their reality. "We're always running, and I'm just... I'm afraid we might already be what we fought against."

Reed holds her gaze, a brief but tangible tether in the chaos that surrounds them. "We'll figure this out, Miranda." Those words hang heavy, burdened by the gravity of their journey—a path convoluted by the specters of their orchestrated past.

Another lurch shudders through the plane, momentarily diverting their attention. Miranda's muscles tense with the instinctual need to brace against an internal storm matching the turbulence outside. Successfully subduing the sleeper agent, she's aware that the only control she has left is over the present moment, and even that feels tenuous at best. Yet beneath the surface, a stronger resolve builds from fractured layers of doubt—an inner promise to defy The Warden's reach however she can.

Settling back into the seat, the plane levels, steadying against the roaring winds. The sudden calm is almost disorienting, and for a moment, the oppressive churning in her mind quiets. Miranda allows herself to breathe, clutching the hope that they've stabilized their path, if only temporarily. But even in moments of respite, The Warden's shadow remains—a specter of unseen threats, casting doubt on the very notion of freedom she so desperately seeks.

In the stillness, she opens her eyes to the steel-clad cabin, a cocoon cradling them from the world outside. The quiet after the chaos is deceptive, rampant thoughts swirling with questions unanswered. Each carries echoes of the past, a puzzle piece pointing to a larger, unseen design. Somehow, some way, she'll unravel it all.

The Zurich Gambit

As the wheels hit the tarmac, the cargo plane shuddered, a groan of relief shared by its passengers. Miranda Carter leaned back in her seat, the adrenaline from their flight seeping slowly out of her system. Zurich rose to greet them, a city of serene promise against the chaos of the past night's escape from Tehran. Yet her heart remained a coiled spring, ever cautious. Their landing may have been smooth, but they hovered far from safety's embrace.

Beside her, Reed shuffled in his seat, his gaze scanning the airport through the window. "We should move fast," he said, his voice low, urgency simmering beneath a veneer of calm.

Miranda nodded, pulling her mind into focus. As they made their way across the tarmac, the Swiss precision of their surroundings contrasted sharply with the erratic tempo of their thoughts. Project Morpheus lingered like a shadow, always within reach. Her resolve tightened—she had to unravel its financial strings, expose the web that fed its monstrous reach.

Once inside the terminal, the duo found a quiet corner to regroup. The efficiency of Zurich Airport spoke of order, the kind that she had come to distrust. They settled at a small bench, whispering strategy amidst a backdrop of sterile calm.

"I'll start with the banks," Miranda began, her voice a thread of determination. "If we can trace the funding, we can pull this thing apart from the inside."

Reed's eyes met hers, skepticism lining the edges of his expression. "And how do you propose we access those kinds of records? Everything will be tightly secured. This isn't a small operation we're talking about."

"I have contacts," she replied, her tone firm but slightly defensive, a hint of the internal struggle he sensed more often these days. "We just need to know where to look."

A pause hung between them, laden with unspoken fears. For every day they fought, the cost grew—another mark on their psyches, another reason to question their choices. But backing down was not an option; the stakes were too high.

"What if we can't do it?" Reed's voice softened. Though his distrust wasn't directed at her, the weight of doubt strained their partnership, hanging over them like an unshakable fog. "They'll be ready for us. And if we're wrong—"

His words trailed off. In them, Miranda heard echoes of her own worries, the uncertainty of battling shades of their own reflections.

She inhaled sharply, brushing away the lingering doubt. "Then we find another way. We've made it this far, and I don't plan on giving up now."

Reed offered a faint nod, resigned yet supportive. The plan was formed, yet the path they walked felt like a tightrope stretched across a yawning chasm. Between them, the silent acknowledgment of shared struggle tightened the bond they relied upon, fragile but unbroken.

Glancing around, Miranda let the airport's mechanical hum absorb her fears. Her thoughts drifted, speculating on the deeper implications of what they might discover. Exposing the financial framework of Morpheus would dismantle more than just a corrupt project—it would unmask facades and bring hidden truths into harsh daylight. But would it suffice to mitigate the threat truly? Would unearthing these secrets mean deliverance, or merely shift the battle deeper underground?

Standing, Miranda motioned for Reed to follow. "We need to keep moving. Let's find a secure location and start digging."

Together, they filed past oblivious travelers, blending into the airport's tide. Each step deeper into Zurich carried them further into the unknown, where answers lay buried beneath layers of deceit. Miranda's resolve sharpened, forging ahead. Despite the temporary calm Zurich offered, the specter of Morpheus lingered, waiting patiently in the shadows.

Chapter 6

The Vault of Secrets

Threshold of Shadows

Miranda Carter stands in the shadow of a Zurich alley, the weight of expectation pressing heavily on her shoulders. Her breath, shallow and even, puffs visibly in the chill morning air. Alex Reed adjusts his collar beside her, a silent promise of the trust they have forged in moments of desperation and revelation. Together, they are on the precipice of another truth in this city of secrets.

Their surroundings hum with a deceptive calm. The rhythmic click of heels and the faint shuffling of feet pass by the alley entrance, oblivious to the impending breach of the bank's veneer of safety. The duo review their falsified credentials, a frayed lineup of papers and whispers of borrowed identities, ensuring the faces they wear will withstand scrutiny.

"Ready?" Reed's voice is low, steady—a man accustomed to weighing cost against duty.

"As I'll ever be," Miranda responds, a steely resolve cloaking any tremor in her tone. The proximity to another piece of her enigma strikes fear deep into her core—a fear that never quite relinquishes its grip, no matter how intrepid she proves herself to be. The clandestine impact of Project Morpheus claws against the walls of her mind, its fingerprints etched into her psyche through blackouts and fleeting recollections.

With a nod, they merge into the pedestrian flow, their strides purposeful among the throng of suited figures. The entrance to the bank looms, a glass fortress designed to intimidate and protect. Frosted doors glide open with implacable efficiency, swallowing them into a world of polished marble and chrome where status is whispered through muted tones and guarded exchanges.

Miranda swipes her card, the access point welcoming her assumed persona with a blink of affirmation. Inside the polished walls lies the promise of answers both terrifying and inevitable. She steps forward, shadowed by Reed's silent vigilance, their pace syncopating as they pass bustling bankers en route to another day of fiscal subterfuge.

The elevator awaits like a metal sentinel, its reflection catching the glint in Reed's eye—a promise of tension to come. Miranda presses the call button with a deliberate calm, desperation tinged with determination simmering beneath her surface.

"What if they find out who we really are?" Reed muses aloud as the door slides shut, enclosing them in glass and steel.

"We've come too far to turn back now. We have to take that chance." Her reply is automatic, yet threaded with the gravity of choice—the choice to walk this razor edge between past hauntings and future revelations.

As the lift descends, the thrumming beat of the building's heart matches her own. The confines amplify her thoughts, echoing the fear of her possible past—conjured from illicit whispers, hushed experiments, and shadowed thrusts into Morpheus' clandestine domain.

Security greeted them in silence when they entered, yet the absence of attention leaves Miranda unsettled. A million unanswerable questions claw at her resolve. Were they known? Would the yawning chasm of memory rear its head again, devouring any hold she has on what she feels is true?

There is no choice but to delve deeper. To uncover what spirits of her past linger among records of erased identities and forgotten duties. The elevator shudders to a halt. The doors sigh open. They step out.

Miranda inhales deeply. The air is antiseptic, with the subtle fragrance of archived history and controlled environments. It is the air of secrets and forgotten ghosts —exhalations whispering of those who once walked these halls, unknowingly tethered to the marionette strings of Project Morpheus.

And yet, fear sparks determination. These shadows no longer hold purchase over her identity. Here, in these corridors of mummified memories and recalibrated fates, Miranda carves ahead. With Reed at her side, she steps forward to plumb the depths of this engineered oblivion, knowing only one truth: she must find these threads, even if they unwind into the tapestry of her own past.

Echoes in the Archive

Miranda enters the dimly lit sublevel, her hands brushing against cold rows of data modules lining the walls like sentinels. The metallic tang of the underground air clings to her clothes, mingling with a palpable tension. She moves quietly, a panther among the crypts of Zurich's secrets, her heart a restrained drum in the silence. A lifetime of manipulation rests in these cabinets and folders, waiting to be unearthed.

She sifts through reams of account documents, each a breadcrumb in a trail leading back to the inception of Morpheus. Her history pulses through her mind, tracing back to a time when worlds were shadowed, and agreements whispered in secrecy. Project Morpheus—born as a covert initiative during the Cold War, its tendrils had seeped into the lives of its unwitting subjects, promising control, exacting horror.

Her fingers stop abruptly on a sheet: bank statements for individuals believed to be dead. Her breath catches in her throat. This isn't just another lead—this is validation that the ghosts of Morpheus are far from vanquished. Fear flares inside her, a phantom pain she'd almost forgotten. What if, she wonders, these entries mirror her own lurking ghost?

Hesitant but driven, Miranda reaches deeper into the records, her eyes scanning with surgical precision. And there it is—her own name, a mocking specter among the deceased account holders. The room contracts around her as if the air itself holds judgment. Her throat tightens; reality shifts beneath her feet, leaving a precarious foothold. Could she truly trust her memories when her very identity had been forged by unseen hands?

The past unravels before her, a web of blurred truths. Her recruitment into Morpheus was hidden behind layers of deception and experimentation, each memory a loaded gun pointed at her psyche. Miranda recalls the faces of those she had once rubbed shoulders with—scientists, soldiers, all woven into a tapestry of control and psychological warfare. She'd been a pawn, and understanding now fills her, hard and cold.

She turns to Alex Reed, her voice barely a whisper. "Reed," she calls, urgency sharpening her words. "You need to see this."

Reed's eyes meet hers, narrowing with concern. "What is it?"

She hands him the printout, her pulse a relentless river beneath her skin. "My name is on here, listed as deceased."

He scans the document and then meets her gaze, a flicker of alarm on his face. "How deep does this go?" he asks, his voice laden with the weight of this new reality.

"We've only scratched the surface," Miranda replies, her voice grave with realization. "If my name's here, who knows what else they've hidden? How many others are on this list believing they're living free?"

They stand in somber silence, the enormity of Miranda's past involvement in the Morpheus conspiracy casting shadows over them. Miranda steels herself, drawing strength from the fragments of her exposed history. She's no longer a pawn—she's the one who will forge the weapon to topple the king.

Run in the Shadows

Sirens pierce the air like a wailing chorus of doom, their urgency slicing through the nervous silence that envelops the sublevel like a suffocating shroud. Alex Reed tightens his grip around a sleek leather folder bulging with purloined files, a pivotal piece—perhaps the final piece—in the jigsaw of Project Morpheus. His heart thuds against his ribs, a relentless beat that drowns out the hiss of pressurized doors sealing the bank's secrets. He casts a quick glance at Miranda, whose features are set with determination, yet laced with a flicker of fear. She mirrors his urgency, rifling through yet more documents, her slender fingers trembling ever so slightly against the paper fray.

Memories churn within Reed, a whirlpool of faces—nameless, voiceless victims who might have suffered at his hands while trapped in the nocturnal fog of his own mind. The truth of his past slashes through him like a jagged blade. He wonders silently, agonizingly, if any among them had seen his face, the face he sees now reflected in Miranda's eyes—one furrowed with unspoken questions and haunted by guilt-laden confusion. Here, standing amidst a torrent of noise and fear, Reed wrestles with the bonds of loyalty and duty that bind him to Miranda. Her trust in him feels like a fragile burden he isn't sure he deserves.

Their hands, swift and precise, continue the fevered dance of clinging to whispers—the truth behind Morpheus—brief seconds before the inevitable collision with authority. The wail of the alarms swells into a crescendo, a cacophony akin to the chaos that rages in his mind. The line between just and unjust blurs maddeningly, tested by the stakes they've unwittingly raised with each revelation unearthed.

A sharp command slices through the echoing corridors, freezing Reed in place. A police officer emerges from the dim, nothing but a silhouette amplifying the dread knotting the pit of his stomach. The ringing cry for backup reverberates, urging them into motion, propelling them through shadowed halls where answers and subterfuge waltz together in secrets tightly guarded.

"Come on, we don't have time!" Miranda's voice cracks through his paralysis, sparking a surge of primal instinct to protect, to flee. He snaps out of his abstraction and focuses solely on their escape. Together, they tear down the steel and glass maze, every thud of footsteps behind them amplifying the frenzied urgency to elude capture.

Corner turns, breath ragged and sour in his mouth, Reed finds his voice. "You think we'll blend in once we're out there?"

"We don't have a choice." Miranda clutches the files tightly to her chest, eyes darting towards the looming exit.

The weight of trust is heavy in the air, and Reed nods, feeling the burden of those unspoken words settle into his bones, one trust overlooking another.

Navigating the warren of Zurich's financial district, they seize on each shadow, melding into the chaos of the cityscape beyond the bank's clinical detachment. Yet inside him, a visceral tension persists, doubt feeding on his fear and vulnerabilities alike. He is trapped within himself as sure as within this city, unable to reconcile the shadows of his former self with the man running for freedom by Miranda's side.

Bursting through the glass doors into the mundane din of Zurich, they merge seamlessly into the symphony of mundane humanity—anonymity becoming his greatest ally. They disentangle themselves from fear-addled flight, drawing in the breath of respite that the crowded streets offer.

"Keep moving." Miranda's voice is low, a shared heartbeat grounding them in their fragile haven.

With each step, Reed fortifies the resolve that initially claimed him in a leap of faith. He understands now, more profoundly than ever, that neither past nor programmed righteousness defines him. It's the here and the now—and all it encompasses—that demands his fidelity. No sirens echoing in his ears can undermine that choice.

Café of Fractured Truths

Rain flutters against the cobblestones as Miranda's phone vibrates sharply in her pocket. The message is curt, the words barely visible in the dim light: the old banker has information. Her heart skips, racing alongside the rhythm of her escaping footfalls. She shows the message to Reed as they navigate through Zurich's labyrinthine streets, blending with the faceless crowd. Their destination—a secluded corner café—is her only focus, each step throbbing with urgency.

In the café, shadows cling to the walls, a haze of whispers hanging between patrons oblivious to the escalating danger outside. The banker is hunched in a corner, his body seemingly molded into the chair as if he might disappear any moment. His eyes flicker with a skittish fear that Miranda recognizes too well. She slides into the seat across from him, noting the shaking of his hands wrapped around a cup far too full for his grip.

As Miranda leans in, the banker beckons them closer, words bubbling up like a last confession. "The Warden," he gasps, breath labored, eyes darting to the exit as if expecting specters, "he's...he's always been in control." His voice is a tremor of revelation, threatening to falter before revelation can reach its full weight.

Miranda feels the weight of countless nights spent in the shadows of Project Morpheus. The reality that she has been a pawn in a convoluted strategy, manipulated to serve invisible masters who pull strings while cloaked in anonymity. The notions of freedom and autonomy blur into nothingness, snippets of a life once held as an exemplar of independence now corrupted by forces wielding illusion as a weapon.

Suddenly, the banker clutches at his throat, his words strangled into silence. Venom surges through him, unseeable yet potent. His collapse is like the gentle falling of leaves, silent yet final. Panic erupts around them; chairs scrape loud protests against the floor, and conversations fracture into startled cries.

Reed's grip hardens around her arm, their shared glance an unspoken understanding that the café is no longer safe. She can feel the tendrils of menace closing in, the oppressive air thick with the threat of unseen hunters, the poisonous whispers of a network that transcends their immediate reality. They bolt from the café, slipping into the drizzle-dampened streets like shadows disappearing into deeper shadows.

The alleys are their refuge, a cold embrace that masks their retreat while adrenaline shines bright and furious in the background hum of the city. They know their anonymity is fragile, yet for now, it shelters them from the tightening noose. The cunning web of Project Morpheus echoes within Miranda's thoughts—it estuaries through unseen channels, sculpting fear and control while the world turns oblivious. Each step further marks their resolve, knowing full well the chimerical nature of the truths they seek—fugitives on the fringe of an unfathomable deception.

Miranda steadies her breath, forcing herself to compartmentalize the dread somersaulting in her gut. Yet, with each stolen glance at Reed, a tether to reality remains; a shared mission alive with urgency, forged from a mutual past now fuel for their uncertain future. Together, they vanish into the ebb and flow of Zurich's enfolding chaos, each stride an implacable pursuit of the elusive truth.

The Warden's Ultimatum

Miranda sits on the frayed edge of a hotel bed, feeling the cramped room fold around her like a cocoon. The room is sparsely furnished, shadows collecting in corners where the flickering light from a lone lamp cannot reach. Beside her, Reed's presence is solid, a tether to reality as she balances the retrieved laptop on her knees. The device thrums to life reluctantly, a piece of machinery with its own secrets to unveil.

Her fingers dance over the keyboard, navigating the scrambled depths of digital barricades. Technical hitches delay their progress, the screen freezing in moments of half-formed replies, as if resisting the knowledge it contains. When Miranda finally succeeds, the file reveals itself with a reluctant flicker—an encrypted video queued for their viewing.

The image that illuminates the screen is unmistakable. The Warden, embodied in his trademark blend of smugness and self-assurance, peers out at them, a visage of calculated control. His voice seeps from the laptop's speakers, a serpent's whisper curling into the room. "Impressive, Miranda. You've arrived at the doorstep of the inevitable," he states, his tone imbued with sardonic admiration, as though applauding a well-executed game.

Miranda shivers despite her resolve, the Warden's digital apparition melding into past encounters. His voice carries the weight of unfulfilled ambitions, echoing the political landscape he manipulates. In his world, alliances shift like sand under him, a testament to his cunning application of power, ever weaving new threads in a fabric of control he deems unbreakable.

She watches the video unfold, the edges of her mind fraying with memories stitched together by the Warden's meticulous hands. He is not just a senator; he is the invisible sculptor molding the fate of political rivals and pawns alike. Under the guise of governance, the lines of national security bend to his sovereign will, compromising ethical boundaries with every decision he enacts. His influence burgeons unchecked, fostering a climate rife with dread for those who dare stand in defiance.

The Warden pauses, his gaze penetrating even through the screen, as if mocking Miranda's past endeavors. "You think you're ahead, but you're not even on the board," he taunts, a challenge dressed as warning, brimming with the knowledge of secrets held just out of reach. His smirk is a reflection of emboldened narcissism, the product of years spent in shadows, underestimated and overlooked. In those recesses, he cultivated the ambition that now festered into a need for validation—a testament to decades spent proving his strength.

Miranda glances at Reed, his silhouette somber against the low light. The room grows quieter, each tick of the distant clock a reminder of the narrowing path ahead. The Warden's taunt lingers, a specter of their past encounters dictated by psychological warfare—each one a step closer to dominance.

The screen fades to black, leaving behind only the static of after-image in the dim space. "He's always ten steps ahead," Reed murmurs, embodying the same sense of looming peril that wraps around them. Miranda, silent in reflection, recognizes the breadth of the Warden's reach —as formidable as it is insidious. Beyond the man's steely façade lies an empire sustained by the craving for perpetuity, a relentless pursuit to dominate every facet of existence.

Surrounded by silence, the oppressive air in the room thick with unspoken fears and ambitions, Miranda acknowledges the unequivocal truth: The Warden remains a rival steeped in elusiveness, ever orchestrating from afar. Meanwhile, their resolve tightens into a vow, not just to unravel the lattice of deceit but to confront this specter of governance with newfound veracity.

Amidst those shadows, a shift occurs—a call to action, cemented by a friction born from shared history and alliances forged in adversity. She knows they must move swiftly, no longer mere spectators to the grand performance The Warden directs. Miranda closes the laptop with delicate certainty, the sound echoing like a gavel marking a declaration of war; they are ready to confront the enemy that knows too much of manipulation, both political and personal.

The Moscow Directive

With foreboding anticipation hanging heavily in the air, Reed watches as Miranda deftly works her way through the labyrinthine files on the old laptop. Her fingers fly across the keyboard, each keystroke holding the weight of potential revelation. His eyes scan the room—a temporary hideout in this corner of Zurich—its sparse corners filled with shadows that seem to claw at the walls, reflecting the insidious network they're piecing together.

Miranda's breaths are steady yet rapid, each exhale hinting at the turbulent whirlpool of emotions she conceals beneath her calm surface. The world around her blurs, every detail of the room fading into insignificance as she deciphers each digital line—a cryptic connection here, an encrypted note there. Finally, she pauses, her gaze narrowing at the screen as a list of Russian prisoners tied inexplicably to Project Morpheus flickers into life. The screen illuminates her face with a pale glow, casting shadows that dance across her features, shadows echoing those in her mind.

The details hidden within the files suggest vast webs spun across continents, unseen puppeteers tugging threads connected to Moscow—a city notorious for its enigmas and veils. High-profile figures loom large in the backdrop of this conspiracy, reminders of the immense forces that may lie ahead, and as each line on the screen is revealed, the already weighty stakes multiply.

Reed shifts slightly, aligning his focus with Miranda's, their shared space thrumming quietly with the knowledge of the enterprise they've undertaken. A palpable tension vibrates through the air, fraying his edge of rationality. "This can't just be coincidence, Miranda. You know that, right?" Reed's voice penetrates the strained silence, his words tinged with the same blend of skepticism and conviction that they share. "Going to Moscow might be exactly what they want us to do."

Miranda's eyes dart towards him, their familiar seriousness cloaked in layers of unspoken fears and unyielding determination. Yet she reads the concern etched across Reed's brow, every bit of doubt and caution reflected back into her own guarded expression. The unknown paths intertwining within the pixels on her screen seem endless, each urging them towards an uncertain fate. Yet undercurrents of resolve begin to stir inside her—a deep-set compulsion that nothing can quake.

"We can't let it stop us," she says, her voice firm. "If there's any chance of getting ahead of whatever they're planning, we need to act now. Whatever this is, it's too big to ignore."

Reed taps his fingers against the table, his mind racing through the potential trap before them, yet his instinct to push forward overrides. The murmur of Zurich outside their window underscores the looming confrontation—the inevitability of treading into waters steeped in conspiracy, where every ripple has vast implications.

"We've already come this far," he finally concedes, picking up the latent challenge carried in Miranda's vow to continue. His mind traces the repercussions, the spiraling complexity woven through their every move since this began. "Let's make sure we're not walking blind."

They lean over the laptop once more, Miranda nodding as she processes the network of digital connections, the ghost of old secrets whispering silently through the ether. The glow of the screen illuminates their decision, sealing away their doubts as surely as they pack up their equipment. A final check of the files, one last moment to envelop themselves in this cloistered corner of Zurich before stepping into the yawning unknown.

As they close the laptop, the murmur of inner voices give way to action. With each gear secured, each fleeting apprehension recognized yet set aside, pipes a murmur of readiness for what Moscow might unfold. Between them lies an unspoken compact—an understanding that this path forward harbors lineages of unseen power and silent danger, yet it calls out to them insistently.

They gather their belongings with purpose, each movement precise and measured, the air steeped in anticipation. Who they are—who they might become—hangs poised amidst the dance of shadow and light, propelling them ever forward. Into the night they go, framed by a city that merely arches a brow to their passing, unaware of the global implications nestled between them.

CHAPTER 7

THE WARDEN'S ORDERS

Shadows at the Moscow Café

The clinking of cutlery and a hum of chatter envelops the Moscow café as Miranda and Reed step through the door. Every face in the crowded room is just one among many; potential threats hide behind casual expressions. The back-corner table is where they focus their attention, recognizing Dmitri Volkov with a subtle nod. His darting eyes, trained on every entry and exit, reflect a tension that mirrors their own, bracing for the unknown.

As they slide into chairs opposite Volkov, the air between them thickens with unspoken anxiety. He leans forward, shadows accentuating the lines of stress etched into his face. The city outside is a blur of gray movement, but the moment stills inside the café; it's as if the walls draw closer, making way for the weight of his words.

"Project Morpheus," Volkov begins, voice low, only just cutting through the ambiant noise. Every word is tentative, revealing a world built on secrets. "They've embedded sleeper agents, everywhere. In places of power —offices, governments, shifting the balance at will." Miranda's fingers tighten around her cup, the implications chilling her more than the icy Moscow air.

Her mind races, tumbling through memories tangled with betrayal. Project Morpheus had been an enigma shrouded in her subconscious, but the reality unfolds painfully clear: a charade woven with strings of innocence turned weapons of chaos. Nations, once stable, now teeter on precipices, destinies manipulated by unseen hands. World leaders they believe safeguarded are mere pawns, orchestrated to dance to a sinister tune if the command is ever given.

Few realize the truth—she herself had brushed the edge of oblivion. To her, the idea had been nothing more than a nightmare conjured in stress-filled dreams. But knowing it now as more than just a haunting illusion breeds a fear rooted deep, threatening the fragile tether holding her reality together. As Volkov speaks, it's not just the global stage she envisions but her place upon it, once unwittingly cast in this grim theatre. An overwhelming urge to dismantle the pillars of Morpheus surges through her, tempered only by the shadow of becoming ensnared again. Can she fight the puppeteer and not the strings, or is she eternally tied to this performance?

Reed's voice breaks through, returning her to the present. "We've seen some of it, but the depth—they're in deeper than Pentagon filings show."

Volkov's reply shivers over the table. "Deeper than any of you know. It runs underground—a network thriving where politics blind the truth."

Miranda nods, sharing a silent agreement with the man across from her. Despite the fear clawing at her insides, she acknowledges the war they must wage is one they cannot retreat from. A part of her whispers, vigilant, warning against the seductive ease of oblivion. She has a choice: fade into anonymity or confront the puppet masters dictating her fate.

As the conversation meanders through whispered revelations—toppling governments, coups hidden behind bustling economies—she feels it; a subtle shift in reality as her peripheral vision blurs, dulling the colors of the café. It's a descent into a void tangible and yet unreal—a blackout both suffocating and freeing. Her consciousness loosens its grip, Reed's face distorting into spectral echoes. With volition no longer her own, she slips, thoughts scattering like leaves in a windstorm.

Internal conflict rises, invoking an -inner litany: *Not now, not here.* The futility of resistance mocks her resolve. From deep within the engulfing void, a question taunts: is she fighting an enemy outside, or is the true adversary lurking within?

Cacophony of Chaos

Reed's voice penetrates the fog enveloping Miranda's mind, a persistent murmur dragging her from the depths of her blackout. Ethereal wisps of light dance before her eyes as she surfaces, unsure of what transpired mere moments ago. Her vision sharpens, revealing the cafe's modest interior humming with the chatter of unwitting patrons. But the crucial details—what led to this overwhelming darkness—slip beyond her reach. She blinks rapidly, strands of Reed's urgencies breaking through the last of the haze.

As awareness floods back, a chilling realization strikes her core: she was poised to harm Dmitri Volkov, her hands feeling weapon-heavy in an empty, stark memory that refuses to click into place. Reed's grip on her shoulder tightens, anchoring her to the present, his own shock evident. Miranda's confusion intertwines with a menacing undercurrent, seeping through the veneer of normalcy surrounding them.

The world around them snaps into disarray. An FSB officer's silhouette pierces the cafe's gentle ambience, morphing into a figure of stark violence. Chaos erupts as the officer's gun barks a merciless ferocity, and Volkov jerks before crumpling from his chair, a marionette severed from its strings. The agent's firearm spells madness, transforming the familiar clanking of utensils into a symphony of terror.

Reed reacts instinctually, hauling Miranda beneath the obscure safety of a wooden table. Her heart thunders in her ears, competing with the scream of chairs scattering and shouts giving birth to pandemonium. Those around them scatter like flustered starlings, crashing against tables and chairs in their blind panic.

Time fractures into isolated moments, the grain of the cafe's flooring whispering against skin as Miranda rights herself, raw urgency pounded into Reed's every motion. He shoulders the chaos with unflinching resolve, shielding her from the jagged maw of violence as they claw towards escape. The air is viscous with fear, and each breath is a battle to remain unseen by the eyes lurking beyond the scene.

Under a cacophony of shrieking sirens, they scramble upright. Tables overturn in their wake, fragments of ceramics underfoot crackling seditiously. Reed urges

Miranda forward, his voice a thread weaving through the tangle of cries and shattered composure.

Navigating a torrent of racing bodies, each vying for sanctuary, is like swimming against a relentless, terror-driven current. Reed angles their path through a tightening warren of retreating patrons. A glimpse of freedom beckons—a doorway framed by the rippling blur of alarm—and their determination to breach it grows fierce. Iron and adrenaline copper the air, ghosting against Miranda's resolve as she stays lockstep with Reed, their flight reduced to a focused drive toward preservation.

"Come on!" Reed's insistence surges above the din, pulling her fully into the throes of their desperation. The world beyond the cafe looms nearer with each harried step, its promise tinged by the awareness of relentless pursuit and the shadows threatening to overtake them.

The rupture of glass and voice blurs into a backdrop of disbelief as the last of the cafe's patrons spill into the chaotic Moscow dawn, and with them, Miranda and Reed tumble into uncertainty—a brief pause before the inexorable pursuit of destiny resumes.

Corridors of Suspicion

Reed ducks beneath an ancient archway, Miranda a step behind, each footfall echoing like a ghost in the dim silence of Moscow's back alleys. Pulses thunder in their ears, battling the wail of distant sirens. Breath plumes in the frigid air, and Reed's thoughts dart like fleeting shadows—rapid, disjointed, laced with uncertainty. How had their carefully orchestrated meeting turned into chaos? He can't shake the image of Volkov, slumped and lifeless, as the memory gnaws at his resolve.

He spares a glance back, not for the pursuing officers but at the figure keeping pace by his side. Miranda appears as shaken as he feels, eyes wide with the same haunting question: Could she be trusted, or was she simply another cog in this deadly game? Self-doubt eclipses everything, whispering insidiously, conjuring specters of implanted directives and a past manipulated by others.

They tumble into a side alley, the dim light casting monstrous shadows on brick walls. Reed braces himself against the damp, cold surface, taking ragged gulps of air. He senses Miranda's presence beside him, a constant reminder of the duality he wrestles with—her as both ally and potential threat. The reality of Volkov's betrayal fans his distrust like embers in a gale.

"Do you even know what that was back there?" The words leave his lips rough-edged, barbed with accusation and fear. Volkov's waning life had left a stain that wouldn't easily scrub away. "How do I know this isn't some elaborate trap?"

Reed searches her face, seeking cracks in the facade that might betray her true intentions. Instead, Miranda's response is a cocktail of defiance and frustration, each syllable a rebuttal to the shadow of doubt he casts.

"At least trust me enough to know I want to end this nightmare as much as you do," she snaps back, anger rising to meet his distrust. Her gaze meets his, challenging him to see beyond the haze of suspicion.

Reed's doubts swirl, a maelstrom of misgivings, enriched by the realization that his perception might be tainted by the very programming they fight against. What if she's not the one being deceitful? What if he's the unwitting antagonist in their narrative?

Their eyes briefly lock: hers shimmering with something akin to vulnerability—a promise wrapped in an unspoken plea. For a moment, the specter of loyalty flickers like a distant beacon.

Sirens wail in earnest; they ripple through the air, urgent, insistent. Somewhere, an authoritative voice barks commands, urging them closer to their grim fate. The radio squawks out news of their guilt, their false branding by Russian authorities. No refuge in this shadowy expanse, no time to process their splintered trust.

"Time to move," he urges, voice hushed but firm, the mantle of responsibility falling heavily on his shoulders again.

She nods, a sharp jerk of her chin, and together they slip further into the dark labyrinth of Moscow's underbelly. Reed's internal chaos lulls into a rhythmic drive to focus, to regain control in the face of his fractured identity.

With every step, the alley's shadowy embrace swallows them whole, masking their retreat. Like prey pursued through a predator's domain, they navigate this perilous dance, eyes unblinking against the threat of capture. Despite the persistent tension, Reed gets a nagging sense that understanding Miranda's journey might mirror his own, a shadow cast on mirrored intentions. With each desperate breath, he grapples with the lingering question:

can they manage to trust each other enough to survive what comes next?

Labyrinth of Midnight Shadows

Midnight drapes the streets of Moscow in a cloak of shadows, their oppressive weight bearing down on Miranda as she ducks into a narrow passageway. The city's expanse seems determined to trap her and Reed within its cobbled embrace, every step off the main thoroughfare like navigating a maze designed by unseen enemies. Her mind races, weaving through the tumult of past decisions and future uncertainties. "We can slip away through an intelligence smuggling ring," she suggests, her voice a rushed whisper against the city's low hum. It's a desperate plan, grasped from the murmurs of an underground world she hoped she'd left behind.

Reed, cautious eyes scanning the shadowed alleyways, tenses. "Can we trust them?" His voice carries skepticism, a reminder that among their dwindling list of options lies the potential for betrayal.

She understands his doubt—every shadow in their world teems with threat. But the urgency of their predicament outweighs caution. "We don't have a choice," answers Miranda, a silent plea woven into her words. Reed nods reluctantly, the tension between them mirroring the city's cold, calculating grip.

As they pace through one dim corner after another, Miranda's thoughts turn inward, brushing against the fragments of her past cloaked in secrecy. Flashes of being thrust into Project Morpheus haunt her—the pressure, the manipulation, the loss of autonomy. Each memory is a shard, piercing through the fragile armor she's built around her identity, leaving her to question whether erasing that past would bring solace or erase the very fabric that holds her together.

Her involvement in the project was born from a chess game played by puppeteers. She was plucked from the sea of the unsuspecting, molded into an unwitting operative. Rigorous training and psychological conditioning shaped a person she barely recognizes—a shadow coiled in the recesses of her mind, surfacing whenever she falters, whenever she doubts who she is without their influence.

The specter of her past gnaws at the edges of her consciousness, dovetailing with the terror of her current plight. Would embracing oblivion bring redemption, peace? Or would it merely strip her bare, leaving nothing of substance behind? The answers are elusive.

"Meeting's set," Reed's voice cuts through, sharp with urgency. The arrangement with the smuggling contact is hastily made, the air crackling with the risk of their gamble. Each step towards the rendezvous point is laden with trepidation, the shadowy confines of Moscow offering scant refuge.

They edge back towards a hideout, peering out from a sliver of light cast by the moon. Below, agents prowl systematically, their trained eyes sweeping the streets, scanning for fugitives cloaked in invisibility born of anxiety and desperation. The walls they move between seem to close in, urging them onward and away, like phantoms slipping through the thin fabric of night.

Miranda's thoughts wander to escape routes. Could they conscript this connection into a pathway towards safety, or are they merely stepping into another web spun by their enemies? Each possibility carries weight, pulling her deeper into doubt, teasing the boundaries of trust she has reluctantly awarded allies during the fight against Morpheus. Her lip trembles slightly, and she presses on, determined.

The streets wrap around them like a living organism, shrinking, expanding, intent on suffocating their efforts to breathe freely. For now, there is no certainty, no promise of safety. There is only movement, driven by the need to flee, to hide, to unearth the deepest parts of herself that whisper of survival, and to remain one step ahead of the darkness. As they step back into the night, the path unclear, she carries the scorch of doubt and the weight of her past, propelling her further into her battle between what was and what may yet be.

Reckoning in the Dark

Inside their dimly lit hideout, the weight of Moscow's watchful eyes feels like a physical presence pressing down on Miranda. The room is sparse, shadows pooling like ink in the corners. She rummages through Volkov's scattered possessions, her fingers brushing against a USB drive. An ordinary object, yet it thrums with potential secrets—a lifeline and a noose all at once.

Connecting the drive to her laptop, a fitful hum fills the room as files begin to unfurl across the screen. Miranda's eyes skim rows of data, each line more damning than the last. Here, amidst the digital forest, lies the truth: documents implicating a high-ranking U.S. senator, known only as The Warden. Breath catches in her throat as her suspicion hardens into undeniable reality. The immense machinery of Project Morpheus extends far beyond anything they had imagined, its roots tangled in the upper echelons of power.

As Reed leans over her shoulder to scrutinize the information, Miranda remains locked in her thoughts, balancing between relief and dread. Discovery comes at a cost. The web of control this project wielded is staggering, spanning governments and whispering promises of power wrapped in secrecy. A profound fear grips her—have her own actions unwittingly furthered this insidious conspiracy? Who was she, if everything she believed about herself was crafted by forces she couldn't see, couldn't touch, until now?

The sirens grow louder, echoing through the decrepit building like ghostly heralds of their impending capture. The familiar weight of panic sits heavy in Miranda's stomach. The implication of being ensnared in such a vast conspiracy, linked intimately with players who see lives as pawns, swarms her thoughts. Her mind, a tempest of anxieties, questions her place as a mere cog in this monstrous machine. Was her newfound understanding ironically only another layer of the manipulation she so desperately sought to destroy?

"Can you believe this?" Reed breaks the silence, voice taut with disbelief. "A senator? This changes everything. We knew it went deep, but I didn't expect this."

"It's a nightmare," Miranda agrees, fighting the surge of helplessness. "This isn't just about us, Reed. It's become something much larger."

Reed's gaze hardens. "So what do we do? We can't take on a senator. We need to be smart about it. We can't rush, but we also can't sit here and do nothing. Especially since we're running out of time."

Her resolve crystalizes, fueled by an urgency that bellows against the cage of her chest. "We expose him. Somehow, we must. But first, we have to survive the next few hours. Nothing will matter if they catch us. We can't outmaneuver them if we just wait."

Reed nods. "Let's focus on getting out. We can't let this data fall into the wrong hands."

The urgency transforms their fatigue into fledgling momentum as they scramble to gather essentials. The duality of her journey encapsulates itself in these moments—where certainty was wished, there lay only uncertainty, woven into her identity and shadowing her every step. She breathes deeply, her determination tempered like steel on the anvil of experience.

Yet, as the sirens crescendo into a cacophony outside, Miranda knows the truth: even if they shed thc light upon these corridors of power, some shadows cling to existence with the tenacity of myth, eluding any hope of a dawn. The clandestine specter of Morpheus, painted in human ambition and folly, is far from banished.

Both of them glance toward the exit, their resolve mingled with a grim understanding of the epic proportions of what they've unearthed. As they prepare to slip away into the waiting night, Miranda clutches the drive like a talisman, embodying both hope and the specter of irrevocable change. In this enforced quietude, the echoes of their discoveries loom large—flashing like storm-laden skies over silent graves.

CHAPTER 8

THE REVELATION IN WASHINGTON

Beneath the Facade of Power

In the heart of Washington, D.C., the sun's light glints off the sleek surfaces of the towering government building, an unassuming guardian to secrets veiled in shadows. Miranda and Reed move through its expanse cloaked in the guise of legitimacy, their formal attire a charade as practiced as any stage costume. Deception hums beneath their feet with every step. They slip their forged IDs past security without a hitch, disappearing into the orchestrated chaos of a bustling conference.

Inside, the air is thick with muted anticipation. Conversations swirl around them, layered with veiled tones of bureaucracy and power as nameless players plotted futures in the dim shadows of indirect lighting. Miranda nods politely to the passing faces, each curve of her lips masking the coiled tension held tightly within. Their senses sharpened to the periphery of unguarded whispers, she and Reed find their cue; deftly, Miranda dares a furtive bend beneath the tables set for grand discussions. The concealed surveillance device is planted with precision, a silent witness ready to unveil the clandestine symphony of Project Morpheus.

The world outside fades as they crouch behind the safe embrace of potted greenery. From beyond, words emerge—clipped, precise, laden with import—the very pulse of global stakes. Eavesdropped conversations reveal a blueprint of orchestration: sleeper agents poised to awaken, a testament to machinations bred in shadow and ambition. Each detail unfurled compounds Miranda's internal march: guilt, fear, a drumbeat that resonates with each revelation.

The enormity of their gamble grips her. Everything is suspended on this fragile tether of knowledge gleaned beneath fluorescent witness. To disrupt, to dismantle, all hangs poised on the precipice of discovery. Yet, within her, an unspoken struggle. Losing a defined past, that web of certainty—even warped—terrifies her more than the darkness it held. To erase history might grant freedom, but it could also sever the very essence that anchors identity amidst chaos.

Reed signals with a flicker of motion, Mirroring her resolve behind fern-filled sanctuary. But their respite is brief—for a sentinel of vigilance prowls. The security guard's eyes traverse the assemblies with an intent that ensnares their nerves within a vice grip. Miranda detects the expansion of inevitability, a looming confrontational dance; that is until intuition guides her eyes toward salvation—a narrow, overlooked closet, an unlikely ally.

With unspoken accord, they ghost toward safety, urgency a whisper against the cadence of unintended footsteps. In the pause behind closed doors, Miranda reflects—contemplates the void that utter dissolution of past could bring. What is one to become in the amnesia of erasure? It bids an allure, promise entwined with trepidation.

Their breaths pass noiselessly in union, synchronizing with an environment that conceals far more than it reveals, until the apparatus of authority fades, and the air stills once more. With the feral caution of nature's survivors, the pair slips out and into the world anew. Their departure, nondescript yet deliberate, seals a chapter within this labyrinth of machination—a slight drop of chaos in pursuit of balance.

Outside, the gleam of day echoes its stark promise across their path, a reminder that courage can tether the heart amidst the tendrils of conspiracy. Yet beneath—the question simmers. Should the hand of history be obliterated if it nourishes the foundation of self, however flawed? But with each step on the capital's pavement, Miranda knows their fractured reality still breathes, dictated not by laws of memory erased, but of truths that redefine the shadows in waiting.

Discreetly, like actors leaving the stage, they dissolve into the anonymity of the world outside, unseen and unrecognized. Yet the weight of knowledge clings to them as they vanish, knowing the storm is yet beginning to form on the horizon.

Blueprints of Conspiracy

Clustered in the deep shadows of the room, Miranda and Reed stand quiet and vigilant among the decor designed to dazzle—opulent chandeliers cast fragmented light across a sea of suits, each attendee here under the silvered guise of power. The room hums with purpose, whispering beneath the surface like a snake in the grass, as they observe the unfolding keynote with the eyes of hawks.

Their pulse quickens simultaneously as the screen flares to life, painting a stark presentation across the room. The chill of revelation slices into Miranda. "Ladies and gentlemen, the senator's strategic brilliance," the panelist declares, "has been instrumental in orchestrating Project Morpheus."

Senator William Harrow. The image freezes on his steely gaze, poised and fine-tuned for influence. Power laced through his fingertips, twisted into threads of conspiracy, is laid bare before them. And now, here in this opulent hall, the undercurrent pulses with the acceptance of truths revealed—a morass of malevolent ingenuity.

Miranda's mind spins, icy tethers curling into her consciousness. She stands on a precipice, looking down into the abyss of her past involvements. Her recruitment had been an enigma wrapped in layers of government secrecy. Conversations in dimly lit rooms with men cloaked in shadows and promises had led her into the folds of Project Morpheus. They had built themselves into her psyche, hedged them in promises of protection and progress. Now, the façade crumbles as she realizes her unwitting place in this game engineered by someone like Harrow.

The presentation transitions to a strategic display—red lines spiraling across the globe, the senator's voice echoing through the chamber. "Political obstacles are opportunities," he intones, his strategy unfurling in the wake of those waiting sleeper agents roaming unseen. Locations blur—names attached to destinies that Harrow deems dispensable for the sake of orchestrating power.

Each point punctuated on this map carves deeper into Miranda's core. Her world tilts dangerously, teetering on the brink of an identity she is both part of and apart from. Memories are ripples in the water, jarring her—a twisted reflection of herself in the wake. Can she ever separate the threads they so intricately entwined? The questions weigh heavily as the details of power hidden in plain sight transform into a menacing construct around her.

Reed's breath catches. Though he remains outwardly composed, an undercurrent of disbelief taints his features as the implications crest into the realm of realization. The justice he's pursued, perhaps tainted, intertwined with Harrow's machinations, poses questions of his own morality—a sleight of hand masked within truth and deceit. The dedication to uncovering these demons might have fueled Harrow's engine, and yet, it is all Reed knows to do.

"How do we even fight this?" Reed finally mutters, the dialogue taut and private beneath the collective murmur. His tone carries the strain of grappling with the enormity before them—a world where the lines between good and evil interlace till they all but vanish.

"We have to stop him." Her voice, though steady, reveals the underlying tremor, a battle cry forged from the mingled guilt and defiance coursing through her veins. Breaking beneath the surface of the façade is their path to redemption—facing the Engram of the past, mutating into something fierce to contend with shadows from within and without.

The weight of their realization envelops them in silence as the room fills with scrambled whispers. Miranda understands this isn't merely about politics or tactics—it delves into darker territory, where innocence is caged amongst calculating intent. Harrow's ambitions stretch beyond the dais, past fiscal agendas and diplomatic charm, rooting deep into the very fabric of lives unseen and altered.

Unnoticed, they dissolve into the crowd, stepping slowly backward into corridors tinged by the echoes of machination. Miranda and Reed absorb their revelations, a clear and present danger of what must come next, the room behind them thickening with tension and signals of discord.

Crucible of Deceit

The conference room is a crucible of whispered terrors. Walls of polished oak reflect opulence, yet the air is heavy with fear—a chilling juxtaposition. Reed feels the weight of secrecy coil around the room, a web spun by unseen hands. At the center of it all, a projector screen flickers with the grim truths of Project Morpheus. The world outside, awash in chaos, remains oblivious to the horrors planned within these walls, a theater for psychological warfare. Power is wielded from the shadows, justifying atrocity as necessary for security—a society blind to its moral decay.

Reed intercepts the murmurings of the room, picking out pieces of the puzzle. Sleeper agents, concealed in the fabric of global politics, await orders to strike. Thousands of lives hang in the balance, their fate sealed by an encryption code that unfurls with cach revelation. The scale of the conspiracy sucks the air from the room. Reed's heart drumming against his ribs, propels him into a confrontation with this new reality—a reality that defies the foundations of trust and identity.

His identity fragments as he grapples with his own programming. In the crescendo of panic, each fragment sharpens into clarity. His memory, once a friend, now recalls shadows of a life not wholly his own—a puppet dancing to sinister rhythms, each pose dictated by a master unseen. Who is Reed, beneath the layers of manipulation? The question gnaws at his core, tearing into the fabric of his consciousness. Are his affections for Miranda his own, or strings tied to control him? The fear is insidious, whispering that even his heart might betray him.

"We've got a problem," Reed says, voice low, as they huddle behind the greenery, the leaves a flimsy shield against the growing dread.

Miranda nods, her eyes tracing the lines of the activation sequence projected on the wall. "A worldwide kill switch," she breathes, "We need to act fast."

"Too fast," Reed replies, fingers itching with the urge to act. "We split up. I can draw them away. You find that server room."

"Always wanting the dangerous job," she quips, but beneath the levity, there's tension coiling like a snake.

The plan is clear yet fraught with uncertainty. "I just want to keep you safe," Reed admits, a rare slip of vulnerability. "Let me handle the diversion."

Their eyes meet, sealing their resolve. The weight of the decision hangs heavy, but in that shared gaze, there's an understanding—a promise of return. As they prepare to part ways, Reed feels the tug of something profound, a hope that this choice might redefine his destiny, away from the shadows.

He dashes into the corridor, the enormity of their mission weaving urgency into his stride. Purpose floods him, intertwining terror with fierce determination. Each step a defiance of the identity thrust upon him, the man he is choosing to become—each footfall echoing the war that wages within.

Echoes of a Lost Self

In the dim, secluded office tucked deep within the sprawling government edifice, Miranda stands before a computer monitor glowing ominously in the suffocating silence. Documents are piled haphazardly nearby—an assemblage of whispered secrets and buried truths. Her fingers tremble as they scroll through directories labeled with cryptic codes and clandestine references. With each click, she feels the weight of their implications grow heavier, a grim foreshadowing of what she's yet to uncover.

A rogue file catches her attention: project_training_sequence.mp4. Her heart pounds with a relentless urgency, the rhythmic onslaught breaking the confines of her chest and echoing through her limbs. She hesitates but a moment, then double-clicks the file, the urgency gnawing at her resolve. The screen flickers before revealing grainy images of a younger version of herself—clad in tactical gear, eyes steeled with purpose—

embroiled in rigorous training exercises. This is more than just footage; it's a window into forsaken chapters of her life, chapters she had no idea had been written.

Her breath catches, turning shallow as the scenes unfold with cinematic clarity—an unwelcomed symphony of emotional dissonance. Memories trapped in a tempest of fear and disbelief rage within while the color drains from her face. She sees herself moving through the drills with precision, dutifully following commands that now read as ominous. This isn't the psychologist who sought justice through understanding but a shadow of calculated efficiency. The Miranda who trained here was someone different, someone she had worked tirelessly to bury under layers of denial.

Her heart contorts with an agonizing duality: the Miranda present here and now, whose life is a collection of whispers and disjointed memories, and the Miranda of the footage, forged in the crucible of covert operations. A storm surges within, battling for dominance—identity clashing against identity. She wants so desperately to reclaim who she thought she was, to reaffirm her narrative as victim rather than accomplice. But the images are relentless, each frame another turn of the knife.

The door creaks open behind her, pulling a startled gasp from her lips as Reed steps into the small room, the tension thickening between them like a physical presence.

"You found something?" he inquires, shadow spilling across his face as the hesitant question lingers in the air, a harbinger of present revelations.

"Reed... Look," she replies, motioning to the screen, the haunted look in her eyes telling a story her voice is too choked to express.

He watches the footage, his own disbelief reflected back at her, their shared history now fraught with mistrust and sorrow. Miranda searches his face, hunting for some semblance of reassurance, but his own battles are etched in the lines across his brow. Doubts root themselves deeper into her mind, ensnaring thoughts and perspectives, tangling her past with his presence.

"How are we supposed to trust each other now?" she implores, her voice a fragile whisper beneath the gravity of understanding. The office around them feels smaller, the remnants of erased identities pressing in on all sides.

Reed, his gaze still locked on the damning footage, attempts to bridge the gap carved between them. "We've come this far together, Miranda. We just need to stay focused on what's real—right here, right now."

He reaches out instinctively, a gesture meant to comfort, but she recoils slightly, her fear of the entangled lines of allegiance holding her at bay. The space between them grows colder, more silent than before. Questions of who they are and what they represent hang palpable in the air. Her mind churns, musing on the veracity of their shared struggle, wrapped in layers of manipulation spun expertly by The Warden.

Though Reed's words try to offer solace, betrayal lingers, an unwelcome guest at the table. Her trust wavers ever-so-slightly, a hair's breadth from snapping under the strain. They stand together yet alone, surrounded by shadows of doubt and betrayal, the whispered remnants of a life constructed by unseen hands. In silence, they wrestle with the ache of identities torn asunder, leaving unease to thicken between them like a shroud as they confront their uncertain path forward.

Crossroads of Trust

As Miranda paces the sterile hallways, pieces of her past flicker through her mind like flashes of distant thunder. Those unnerving days when she was groomed into becoming a weapon haunt her now—her identity, once fiercely independent, chiseled away as she was molded by those relentless hands of her overseers. An echo of the doubt that has haunted her ever since grips her heart: Does she truly have the capacity for freedom, or is she perpetually ensnared in shadows, an assassin lurking beneath her skin?

The corridor seems to conspire against her as she reflects on the layers of manipulation she endured under Project Morpheus. The memories are vivid—the cold, clinical spaces, the cadence of authoritative voices stripping her of free will—reminding her how easily they defaulted every impulse to obedience. Yet here she stands, determined to steer her own course, aware that she is more than the sum of another's twisted programming.

Suddenly, The Warden's insidious command reaches Reed, coiling around his mind. A jolt courses through him, as though electrified by the unseen, and he stumbles momentarily, eyes clouding before that glazed focus locks on her. Her heart clenches. In an instant, Reed's gun is drawn, the barrel cold and impersonal. Miranda stands frozen, the hallway's sterile light glinting off the weapon, stark against the chaos she never imagined she'd face so close to him.

“Reed!” she gasps, stepping back as the weight of his aim settles on her shoulders like impending doom. Her voice quavers, entwined with disbelief and desperate hope. He hesitates, his brow creasing as his grip wavers, the battle playing out in the lines of his face.

“Don’t! You know me, and I know you. Remember what’s real!” Her words spill from her heart, unbidden but searing into the pulsating air between them, the sincerity in them a tether to the man she knows hides beneath the artificial commands. She searches his eyes, aching to reach the Reed hidden beneath layers of cryptic programming.

Reed’s gaze flickers, shadows of shared moments and their tenacious quest to dismantle what they thought impenetrable. Standing there, mere feet between them yet caught in a war that seeks to rend them apart, she implores with every fiber of her being, “This isn’t you, Reed. I need you, here with me. Fight this.”

His hand trembles, the muzzle shifting, and time itself seems to expand, each second heavy with uncertainty. The rhythmic chaos echoes around them, a frenzied yet soundless cacophony as both wrestle within the confines of a hall that tightens with urgency and fear.

The interlocking hallways bustle with unresolved tension, every footstep and murmur reverberating with the unknowable breadth of The Warden's reach. Yet here, amidst this spiraling tempest, Miranda stands unwavering —her resolve a flame flickering defiantly against the swelling darkness.

For a heartbeat, hesitation etches itself across Reed's expression, and she recognizes the crack—the fleeting moment where choice confronts compulsion. Their shared history envelops them, a balm to their divisive reality, as he blinks away the storm shadowing his mind.

In the echoes of reassured silence—a silence piercing amidst the simmering chaos—Miranda observes the flicker of humanity returning to his eyes. It kindles an ember of hope, fragile yet fierce, bridging mind to heart with a whispered promise of reclaimed control. Their truths hang suspended between them, regeneration surfacing from the chaos, momentarily whole amidst the madness.

Labyrinth of Control

Chaos unfolds as Miranda becomes ensnared in the clutches of security, their grip unyielding as they corral her through the disorienting warren of corridors. The sharp echoes of their march punctuate each step, mirroring the tumult in her mind. The labyrinthine passageways curve endlessly, the walls flanked by servers humming with ominous portent, whispering secrets she senses yet cannot decipher. She draws a breath, steeling herself against the eerie familiarity that lingers like a phantom limb.

Their path spirals downward, darkness pooling in alcoves like ink spilled upon parchment. Each intersection a tangle of shadows and intrigue, Miranda tracks the subtlest shifts in her captors' movements. These corridors are foreign yet palpably dangerous, the sterile climate-cloaked airs more suffocating than any draconian fortress. She lets her focus widen, searching each fleeting glimpse for keys to their cunning contraption. The deeper they descend, the more she perceives the metaphorical net tightening around her, a serpent coiling about prey.

The journey yields to an unveiling: a chamber sterile as a surgeon's workshop, where the air tastes of antiseptic intent. Screens blossom to life around her—grand yet foreboding—The Warden's presence spilling forth from the mosaic of monitors. His voice, cultivated and callous, weaves through the room like a venomous waltz, tempting, taunting. Each syllable a calculated provocation, alluring in its suggestion of a larger game yet to unfold. He speaks to humanity from atop a pedestal of power and manipulation. Miranda feels The Warden's challenge seep into her marrow, daring her to shatter the carapace of control he's ensnared around countless others.

As his words swirl about her like smoke, Reed becomes her anchor, her inner compass spinning wildly without him. Her mind runs through potential strategies, driven by the passage of dwindling time. Somewhere in the facility's subterranean guts, Reed hunts for the path to reach her, his frantic quest echoing distantly through the air. Miranda fixes on a single thought—a determination fierce as fire—to confront the thoughts draped by shadows and, with Reed, elevate beyond this intricate snare.

Echoes dance down the corridors like a chorus of hauntings, each sound wrapped in the promise of betrayal or redemption. Miranda draws herself up, the turbulent currents within her calming to tides steady and deliberate. With her resolve galvanized, she recognizes these moments—silent but thunderous—as part of an inevitable confrontation, demanding every ounce of resilience she's unearthed throughout this twisted journey. She braces, a warrior poised at the cusp of destiny, ready for the showdown that awaits within these unyielding walls.

CHAPTER 9

THE TRAP IS SET

Chained by Memory

Miranda blinks, trying to focus her vision in the dim, stuttering light, but the shadows shift restlessly across the ceiling like some foreboding dance. Her head is heavy, a swimmer surfacing for air, and yet held fast in a grip of iron—straps circling her shoulders, waist, arms, and legs. The air hums steadily with the drone of technology around her, a mechanical symphony of unseen machines whispering their threats. Immediately, she knows she is someplace underground, buried beneath layers of earth, concrete, and deceit.

The screen before her, larger than she can fully comprehend in this dizzying moment, blinks to life, bathing the room in a cold, authoritative glow. An array of archive files race across it, cataloging—like trophies of a twisted game—moments from a past life she'd rather bury. Her breath quickens as names and dates scroll by, each an unceremonious tally of the lives she extinguished under Morpheus's dark compulsion. Her gaze traces the trajectories marked in red, vivid displays of her own actions, each a story of calculated precision and frozen detachment. The memories rise unbidden: the whisper of silk under her fingers, the darkness of her shrouded targets, the finality of a breathless night.

In that sterile, humming room, The Warden's slick voice echoes from unseen speakers. It cuts through her panic, speaking of purpose, superiority, inevitability. "Consider this homecoming, Miranda," the voice purrs, rich with persuasion. "Embrace your truth or risk oblivion." The declaration hangs in the air: join them, be them, or drift nameless into nothingness, her mind wiped clean as if she never existed.

Reality flares anew, spurred by a mixture of fear and a simmering defiance she thought long buried and dry. The scrap of rebellion stirs, uncoils in her chest, hot and bold against the cold threat encircling her. Miranda knows this game; she's played it, been played by it. Beneath the oppression of metal and mandates, she clings to the ember of autonomy, wills herself to rise above the dissonance of memory and manipulation. The neural interface hums its ominous song, a mechanical reminder of the power held over her, seeking to crush her spark beneath its remorseless wheels.

Project Morpheus reached beyond what she once believed possible. Sleeper agents engineered to shift the levers of power in silence, shape policies with unseen hands, leave fingerprints on the history books hidden in classified ink. Behind the curtain, the government's experiments and ambitions played out like a grand performance, twisting the world in the shadows with psychological warfare—devious vines creeping into the heart of nations and society. A world on a puppet's strings, guided by whispers in the dark and the ethical absence of its true controllers. Miranda's past involvement forms a cornerstone of this narrative, each of her missions another stone laid in the unfeeling edifice of state control.

Inwardly, Miranda twists through her own maze of guilt and anger, festering wounds from a life of sanctioned imperatives—the stabs and thrusts of a puppet pulled along by a master unknown. Memories carve their way through her defenses—the faces of shadows, the fog of voices stripped of identity. She grapples with the idea of herself, torn between what was and what she might still be. The assassin sleeps quietly beneath her skin—a predator subdued but restless, pacing under the moon's light in her mind, demanding recognition. Yet against the anticipation of erasure, she finds herself questioning: can she destroy everything to be free, or is there another path through the darkness?

She gazes at the screen, unwavering in the face of The Warden's threats. Whatever choice she makes next could mean her passage into a life unmarred by Morpheus's taint or a surrender to its grasp. Miranda braces against the flow of panic, the pressure, and the power, harboring her silent defiance amidst the hum of automata. Like a ghost refusing release until its dues are paid, she yearns to carve her own path through the looming shadows, daring the darkness to forget her—or to prepare for a fight.

Tangled Loyalties

Reed stands at the shadowed entrance of the underground facility, cloaked in the cacophony of humming technology and the oppressive heft of imminent decisions. The activation command has drawn him here as surely as if strings were tied to his limbs, tugging him into the web of manipulations spun by The Warden. He glances around quickly, his training overriding the tremor in his hand that betrays a mind wrestling against implanted orders. Small displays flash along the walls, casting a dim, sterile glow across his features as he advances, each step driven by an unseen force yet mired with hesitation.

Stopping outside the chamber, he sees her— Miranda. Restrained by heavy straps, her figure is silhouetted against the luminous screen, her expression etched with both defiance and a flicker of recognition. For a moment, Reed stands motionless, caught in the tide of memories: whispered conversations shared during starlit nights, fleeting touches of comfort exchanged in darker times, moments when they were just two individuals threading through the chaos together. His grip tightens, nails biting skin, as if the pain might anchor him against the roiling sea of orders coursing through his veins. It is a cruel push-pull, loyalty grappling against duty, heart clashing with the patterns encoded deep within his synapses.

Their eyes meet—his gaze tinged with conflict mirrored in her steel-jawed determination. A taunting laugh ricochets off the walls, The Warden's voice twisting around them, weaving barbs into the air. "Two puppets dancing without strings, or so you think," he declares, the words crackling with disdain. The implication of disloyalty settles heavily around them, igniting a defensive edge as if drawn into an invisible arena, combatants tethered by shared pasts and tangled futures.

Miranda's voice reaches out—calm, cutting through the static—aimed straight toward him. "Reed," she begins, raw emotion threading her words together, unfurling the tightly wrapped vulnerability now exposed. "I need you to fight this. We've faced worse, but never alone." Her plea hangs in the air, reaching for the core he has buried beneath programmed reflexes.

The air shifts subtly between them, or perhaps that is the surge of buried emotion, the weave of trust and trepidation dancing on the cusp of eruption. Reed feels it pulse beneath his skin, a tangled mess of memories and loyalty he cannot yet untangle, nor fully betray. They stand there, amidst the metallic hum, the shadows of their past lives interlacing as they brace for whatever treacherous maneuver comes next.

Shattered Reflections

Miranda stands in the midst of sharply defined brightness, the interrogation chamber pressing in with its stark sterility. The intense light castigates her, leaving little room for shadows to hide in. Flashes of past missions flicker across the screen before her, each image stabbing through her consciousness like shards of glass. Fragments of her past—bloodied hands, silent footfalls in dark alleys, and vacant eyes staring back at her—seep into her mind as The Warden's voice drips through the speakers, slick and caustic, painting her with blame and doubt.

Fear chokes at her resolve. She can feel the suffocating grip of her former life as an agent slithering back, threatening to strangle all semblance of autonomy. Betrayal tastes bitter in her mouth, its taste cloying, pulling at her memories of loyalty intertwined with manipulation. She finds herself teetering at the brink of that past life, a yawning chasm of violence and cold obedience.

Miranda had once believed the system could be undone, its threads pulled apart to reveal the truth she craved: a reassurance that she was more than gears in its monstrous machine. Yet, here she stands, confronted by tendrils of her history, urging her back to chains of her design—chains forged in blood and shadows. The battle for identity becomes a thrumming ache in her chest, vibrating with urgency and a hint of defiance.

Reed enters, his presence a raw wound within the room's controlled façade. Memories of shared laughter and soft whispers puncture the air between them, only now they mix with the static hum of a command pulling at Reed's edges, seeking the chasm in his loyalty. Miranda's heart aches as she sees the flickers of their past reflected in his eyes, a war she feels every bit as much as he does.

"You know this isn't you," she presses, her voice sharp yet hopeful as she walks the tightrope between certainty and loss.

Reed's gaze, torn by invisible bonds, wavers. Tears whisper at the corners of his eyes, unspilled remnants of memories that won't settle. "It's like his voice... crawls into every corner," he admits, betraying the flickers of resistance enveloping his struggle.

Miranda leans forward, her voice a fervent whisper, "Remember that night by the river? We spoke of futures, of leaving shadows behind. That was real, Reed. This is not."

Exceptionally fleeing moments cascade around them, the push and pull of The Warden's manipulation and the fleeting serenity of genuine connection. For Miranda, the fear of losing herself—or Reed—to the program's insidious demands is incandescent. Her heart pulses with every word she speaks, becoming a beacon of reminder, of resilience, as past emotions weave into the narrative they share.

Reed blinks slowly, the intensity of their shared history flashing before them like a feverish dream. The Warden's voice, crystal and taunting, tries to bruise their memories, casting doubt on intentions long buried.

"You know what they did to us. Don't let it bury you," Miranda implores, as desperation and courage battle within her. In a room where promises were once made clearer by moonlight, the air now hangs heavy with the possibility of loss and betrayal.

Their eyes lock again—a silent yet fierce confrontation each word relentless, every past promise unfurling in a world standing at the precipice of fate. In this place, where decisions carve deep into the soul, any step forward lies wrapped in shadows of mind games and memories.

Reclamation in the Interface

The dim light of the underground facility flickers erratically, amplifying the echoes of machines buzzing in cold synchronization that permeates the room. Miranda sits restrained in the high-tech neural interface chair, her mind a battlefield as the weight of memories crashes down around her. The straps pressing her skin feel like a grotesque reminder of the chains she once embraced. Her breathing is shallow, each exhale laced with an icy dread that curls through her veins.

A large screen before her illuminates the darkened room, displaying a montage of her past missions in vivid detail. Clips flit past: meticulous plans executed with chilling precision, nameless faces immaculately erased. Illegal deals, stolen blueprints, silent dispatches... Miranda sees herself in those memories, cold and detached, a mere shadow of the person she yearned to become, stripped of emotion and remorse. The Warden's voice looms, dripping with derision. "You'll always be one of us," his voice taunts, echoing a lifetime of indoctrination.

At this moment, Miranda's resolve hardens, an unrelenting determination to wade through the murk of her subconscious mind. Her past dances before her like a mocking specter. Those were the missions that shattered her soul piece by piece. She remembers the trust she misplaced in him, the way she clung to his words like gospel, hoping they would anchor her. How naive she had been—the chains she thought were saviors were little more than shackles in disguise. But now, these memories serve as fuel for her defiance. Her identity, once all-consuming, is now a mere phantom she is intent on erasing.

Within her, something raw and primal stirs, a mental trigger she had buried beneath layers of conditioning and self-denial. She reaches for it, this elusive, stubborn fragment of her true self, allowing it to be her lifeline against the waves of programming that threaten to drown her. The interface hums louder, tightening its grip on her mind like a web spun by some malevolent architect - its design elegant and deadly.

As the confrontation escalates, Miranda locks eyes with the faint reflection on the screen, a face simultaneously familiar and alien, its eyes glinting with tenacity. Holding onto her independence and integrity as tightly as she can, she braces herself against the tide, pushed to her limits but refusing to succumb.

Just behind her, Reed struggles, his own internal tempest mirrored in the storm that brews within her. She can sense his presence, his turmoil; they are separated by more than mere physical space, each battling the phantoms of their own making. Yet, it is in this shared struggle that she finds her strength. It is in this moment of shared defiance that Miranda acknowledges that the fight is far from over.

The facility trembles as a surge of power disrupts the relentless hum, casting volatile shadows that dance across the walls. The chaos swirling within is mirrored by the storm building around them. For an instant, the room is charged with static, as if the very air held its breath—hovering on the precipice between revelation and destruction. And in that pause, in the silence poised like a predator about to strike, Miranda knows: the path to reclaiming her autonomy lies not just in defiance, but in the acceptance of her own fractured, formidable self. She understands that her fight is not merely against The Warden, but with the specters of who she was and who she must become.

Reckoning of Souls

The control hub is a hive of activity, monitors blazing with flashes of red—a forewarning of chaos unfurling. Reed's heart pounds a discordant rhythm under the harsh fluorescent lights. His steps falter, and the air seems heavier, laden with a charge not entirely his own. He lunges toward Miranda, confusion embroiled with resolve, a frail puppeteer pulling at the frayed strings of his consciousness. The jam of electronics, the crackle of a short circuit in the neural interface interrupts the surge, halting him with a jolt.

The moment sharpens. Reed's vision clears as fragments of truth cascade over the manufactured chaos. His breath catches; a veil lifts to reveal an expanse of choices. He's no longer bound to scripts whispered to him in shadowed corridors. In the relentless hum of machinery, he finds a sliver of clarity, a recognition of self previously submerged. The room, filled with impending disaster warnings, seems to warp around him as he clings to the newly discovered agency with a fierce yearning for liberation.

"You remember me?" Miranda's voice breaks through, her weapon lowered, eyes wide with the anguish of shared history. Memories flood Reed's mind—distant echoes of laughter and whispered plans under the yawning sky. Moments that defined a purpose eclipsed by the manipulation of hidden masters. "Remember us?" The words hang heavy, entangled in desperation and fragile hope.

They grapple, both with the proximity of their physical forms and the spiritual distance coerced by The Warden's machinations. Fear and love—two titanic forces—clash within the confines of this room, each seeking dominion over the other. Violence teeters on the brink, yet beneath the surface, memories ply away at layered defenses, seeking passage to the surface.

Miranda contemplates a world unshackled from the scars of Project Morpheus. Her mind forges paths untraveled, inconceivable lives where she might craft an existence untainted by relentless shadow and whispered deceit. Could she sever those relentless chains, find solace in the mundane, build love not born out of fractured secrets? The simplistic allure of an unburdened identity calls to her, promising genuine connections devoid of hidden daggers, yet the price remains uncertain. Her uncertainty tightens cold fingers around her resolve—is she truly beyond the reach of manipulation, or haunted forever by the tendrils of past trauma? Those thoughts braid into a storm within her as she stands grounded in the present confusion.

More immediate turmoil overtakes as Reed hesitates, muscles aching with the strain of his newfound clarity. A silent war rages—past against present, duty against desire—no victor in sight, save those yet freed from consequence. Their eyes lock, bridging an unspoken promise neither has yet vocalized. Together, they dance within the fiery circle of calamity, bordered by oscillating truths and blaring alerts. A collapsed room in spirit, yet not entirely lost—a smoldering reminder of paths unseen and futures unwritten.

CHAPTER 10

THE TRAP IS SET

Inferno of Awakening

Alarms burst to life, an invasive symphony of chaos reverberating through the underground facility. Scarlet lights flash, bathing the narrow halls in an ominous glow as The Warden enacts the devastating plan to activate sleeper agents worldwide. The walls seem to pulse with urgency, confining the panic that simmers through the crisp, sterile air.

Miranda Carter stands rigid for a moment, the alarm's blare a chorus of impending doom. Her gaze finds Reed's, a shared understanding coursing between them—a silent acknowledgment of the catastrophe looming over them and the world outside. Within the confines of this facility, they confront the disheartening truth of Project Morpheus, a shadowy operation reaching its cold, manipulative tendrils into key positions of power, threatening to unleash chaos on an unimaginable scale. A network of sleeper agents, embedded deep within society, awaiting activation to strike—each one a specter of potential destruction. These operatives, groomed to perfection, embody a latent threat to global peace, driven by the puppeteer hidden in the darkness.

Miranda's heart pounds a relentless drumbeat, a physical echo of her own chaotic dread. As she and Reed dart through the labyrinth of dimly lit corridors, her urgency takes the reins. Confrontation is inevitable, lurking around each corner. The flicker of corridor lights casts erratic shadows, whispering reminders of the days when she herself had walked these halls, blind to her own manipulation. The weight of past transgressions threatens her resolve, the chill of her own history brushing the back of her mind with icy fingers. Gripped by both determination and unspeakable fear, she races against time, each step heavy yet driven by the desperate need to thwart the disaster planned by The Warden.

Their path is abruptly obstructed by Morpheus operatives, their faces grim beneath the pulsing lights. The snarled command to halt comes too late; Miranda is already in motion, catching sparks off the cold floor as gunfire blazes between them. She dives for cover, instincts threading survival into the chaos that explodes around her. The polished concrete chills her outstretched fingers, head ducked as bullets ricochet off walls, sending shards of fear splintering through her chest.

"Carter," Reed shouts over the crack and thunder, eyes wide as he presses against the wall. "We can't let them stop us here!"

Miranda nods, steeling herself. "I've got an idea," she replies, her voice tight with tension. Her mind races to piece together strategy amidst the leaden cacophony, sketching out their desperate push toward the control hub and the critical data it harbors.

"Cover me," she calls, her determination as firm as the weapon held tightly in her grip. As Reed raises his firearm, she braces herself, lungs drawing in one more breath laden with the acrid smoke of conflict. They're close now, and yet the distance between action and resolution feels as wide as the chasm between dark and light. In the clamor, Miranda burns with resolve, her heart thrumming the only truth she knows: to face the weaponization of the human psyche, she must reach the heart of Morpheus.

Race Against the Clock

Fluorescent screens flare wildly, their glow painting the control room in a surreal dance of colors, each flicker a reminder of the urgency infiltrating the air. Miranda's fingers blur over the keyboard, her eyes narrowed in focus, the digital interface before her a jungle she has to navigate with expert precision. The backdrop hums with chaos, an orchestra of alarm bells rising as if to warn her of the ticking countdown. But she’s in her element, fingers gliding over the keys like an adept pianist in a critical solo.

Project Morpheus is a festering behemoth beneath the surface of normalcy, its tendrils reaching into every facet of government and beyond. Miranda has seen the reports, aware of how sleeper agents nestle within corridors of power, their existence indefinitely altering the precarious balance of global influence. It scares her more than she admits—the thought that a whisper from The Warden could plunge nations into turmoil at any instant. The potential harm extends beyond just individuals; it threatens the very fabric of societal stability around the world. Knowing this, she feels a steely resolve to drag the conspiracy into the light where it can be cauterized.

"Miranda, how's it looking?" Reed's voice cuts through the din, his silhouette stationed at the door. There's an edge to his words, riding the undercurrent of adrenaline pulsing through the chaos.

"Almost there," she replies, barely glancing up. Each keystroke inches her closer to unearthing the critical list —the marked identities of all sleeper agents, the revelation that could dismantle Morpheus if wielded correctly.

Her cursor halts over a file gleaming ominously: 'All Sleeper Agent Identities.' Miranda's breath catches as she initiates the download. Every second stretches taut, a high-wire she and Reed walk with peril nipping at their heels. She fights an urge to look over her shoulder, trusting Reed's vigilance without question, as the system churns, informing each second ticking by with a sudden, looming clarity of danger.

Miranda's reality is threaded with silent battles—her ongoing struggle with identity an unyielding torment surfacing with every reminder of Morpheus's reach. Though ridding her past seems like freedom, it shackles her with fear, clouding the boundary between releasing her past demons and surrendering a part of her soul. But here and now, her persona is one with purpose, every fragment of trauma stoking the fire that keeps her fingers agile and her resolve unwavering.

A shrill alarm shatters her concentration. The download clicks complete as Miranda seizes the USB like a lifeline, nerves electric under the escalating cacophony. "We've got company," Reed warns, tension wrapping around his words as operatives converge outside.

“We need an exit strategy fast,” Miranda calls back, the thrumming urgency mirrored in her expression as flashing alarms daub them in hues of danger. She swivels on her heels, aware their task is barely half-finished. The operatives are swift on their tail, intent on retrieving what they’ve snatched away from under their noses.

“GO! Get us out of this mess!” Miranda doesn't pause to weigh her words, the urgency acting as her sole guide. Swift on Reed’s heels, the descent into chaos is palpable, a reality they cannot afford to yield to.

As they thread through the labyrinthine corridors, Miranda clutches the USB like a talisman, its precious cargo poised to tip the battle scales in their favor. Each stride is laden with gravity, not just for their survival but for dismantling the web that has ensnared countless lives —a fact neither she nor Reed can afford to lose sight of. In the maelstrom, their resolve crystallizes, chained to the shared purpose that promises an uncertain yet necessary freedom.

Shattered Conscience

Reed clutches the USB file like a lifeline as gunshots and warning sirens pulse around him, seeking refuge in an obscured corner of the control room. The chaos swirls like a living storm, tech displays overhead broadcasting flickering streams of data, as if mocking his fragile grasp on reality. His breathing is ragged, heart pounding against the oppressive weight of his past. In this momentary stillness, the memories he's buried for so long claw to the surface, a torrent of suppressed violence and cold detachment as vivid as the present turmoil.

Faces of those he's hurt flash through his mind—fearful eyes and pained expressions, humanity snuffed out by his own hands under the guise of duty. Guilt crashes over him in suffocating waves. How many lives had he taken without even recognizing their humanity, their silent pleas piercing through his scripted programming? Confusion weaves tighter bonds around his psyche, blurring the boundaries between who he is and the puppet he was programmed to become.

Reed feels his knees buckle beneath the burgeoning weight of his crimes, sinking onto the cold metal floor. His hands tremble, clutching at his sanity, the cracking facade of control crumbling with each punctuated beat of the alarms. The facility's walls seem to tilt and leer, echoing The Warden's sinister laughter—a taunt from where his mind rebels against the cold indifference it was forged into. What is left of him now? The man or the machine, spurred into life by triggers he no longer controls?

Miranda's approach is fast and urgent. Her voice cuts through the dissonance, urgent and grounding, a tether to the world teetering on collapse. "Reed, listen. We don't have time for this—I need you," she urges. Her hands grasp his shoulders, shaking him free of the spiraling darkness threatening to engulf him. Her concern is palpable, yet firm, a reminder of the connection woven through shared battles.

"I'm trying," he chokes out, the words tasting foreign in his mouth. "It's... it's like I can't control it."

"Trust me. We can do this," she insists, her intensity unwavering, her eyes locked onto his. "We need to get out of here. This isn't where it ends for us."

Reed battles internally, clawing through the fog of remorse and habit, Miranda's presence steadying him against the turbulent tide. Her words cut through the background din like essential lifelines, piercing the morass of his identity crisis. Each breath is a decision—a reminder that choice lives within him, not within the whispered orders from a long-gone, twisted master.

Taking a shaky breath, Reed meets Miranda's gaze; her resilience emboldens him. The determination that replaces desperation is a feat of sheer willpower, born anew from kindled embers of self-belief. With renewed focus, Reed pushes himself back to his feet, the USB drive secure in his grip. The sirens scream louder, the urgency undeniable, but now he stands with purpose—a man ready to reclaim his future from the past's shattered remnants.

As Reed and Miranda prepare to move, the facility's screens around them flicker ominously, illuminating The Warden's detached smirk. Confidence exudes from the mastermind's calculated expression, even now taunting them with the notion that their escape is futile.

"Ah, Miranda and Reed. You're still playing this little game?" The Warden's voice trickles from the speakers, icy fingers wrapping around Reed's consciousness. "Trying to outmaneuver me will come at a cost, I assure you."

Miranda stays silent, but the sharp, focused glint in her eyes speaks volumes as she braces for the inevitable, knowing any escape is fraught with danger.

“I’ve prepared a special failsafe, just in case. You wouldn’t want to awake all your ‘fellow’ sleepers, would you?” The Warden chuckles darkly.

Reed and Miranda’s shared glance confirms the ticking clock in both their minds—each second a bead of sand slipping through fateful fingers. The air vibrates, the facility’s integrity cracking like a distant ocean swell starting to crest, debris already falling with the tremor of impending disaster. The Warden’s latest trick amplifies the risk—their determination hardening against the growing odds.

Countdown to Cataclysm

Screens flicker to life around the room, casting harsh, jittery light on the control panels lining the walls. Every surface in the cramped control center seems to vibrate with anxiety, adding to the growing cacophony of alarms. With a grim smile that promises calculated chaos, The Warden's face fills the central monitor. His expression, a blend of amusement and disdain, is a stark contrast to the frantic energy of the room.

"Congratulations, Miranda. Reed. Your efforts, though brisk, are in vain." The Warden's voice, smooth and unwavering, echoes through the facility. His words are heavy, clinging to the air—another layer in an already stifling atmosphere. Each syllable a reminder of the control he wields, a silent promise of dread.

Miranda stations herself within reach of the main console, tension reflecting in the rigid lines of her posture. The Warden's next words send a cold shiver down her spine. "But all good things must come to an end. I must remind you that your escape is hardly assured. Shall you proceed with it, you will witness the rebirth of every sleeper agent in range, stirring them from their slumber."

Reed catches Miranda's eye. She can feel the weight of their shared realization hit like a physical blow—a sickening certainty in the pit of her stomach. Every second that slips through their fingers inches closer to catastrophe.

"He's bluffing," Reed mutters, a hint of doubt shading his voice. But Miranda sees through the veil of bravado in his words. Somewhere deep inside, she knows the clock is ticking, each ominous tick a pulse beneath her skin.

The room reverberates with a low growl as the floor beneath them trembles subtly. An unnatural graze trembles through the concrete, touching every surface with whispered malevolence. Above, particles trickle from the ceiling—a thin stream of dust marking the birth of deeper fractures to come.

Miranda contemplates the enormity of the threat The Warden holds over them, her mind racing as she calculates every possible outcome. The sleeper agents, scattered like seeds across the globe, each one poised to bloom into violence at the behest of a faded smirk on a screen. Her breath catches. Could she risk it? Allow herself the chance at true agency by risking so many innocent lives?

The oppressive grip of fear reaches into the deepest parts of her mind. Yet among that fear is a flicker of fierce defiance—an ember that has refused to be snuffed out. If she can't smash apart the very chains binding her, if she has to bend, let it be to gather the wires, the exposed nerves igniting within her, fuse them into something unstoppable: determination.

They have come too far and lost too much to finish it here. It can't be the end—she won't allow it. Haughty satisfaction twinkles in The Warden's eye like a bare nerve, dangerous to touch. His presence is visceral, a taunting reminder of the power he assumes. But power, she recalls, can fade. Even gods fall when their empires crumble. Maybe, just maybe, her own freedom lies not in erasure, but in breaking what has bound them.

The facility's very bones groan as another shudder travels through the corridor, knocking more dust loose in swirls around them. Watching, waiting, Miranda and Reed exchange one last nod of understanding. Reckoning pulses between them—a need to act, a mutual binding resolve, now etched into the marrow.

The crack in the ceiling widens with a deafening groan, releasing a cascade of debris in its wake. Urgency propels Miranda forward as she rethinks their approach, determination simmering beneath her skin, each heartbeat echoing in time with the rumbling around her. The Warden watches—a spectator, an orchestrator of chaos.

A final smirk passes between them, fed by the creeping realization of what must be done. Together, Miranda and Reed gather strength, the ruin around them spurning them onward. The cost of their escape won't be found in fear—it lies in the resistance they forge, here and now, against the shadows that threaten their world. The only way out is forward.

Chasing Daylight

The facility pulses with an eerie, flickering glow as Miranda's eyes dart frantically through the haze of smoke and debris. The chaos is electric, every nerve afire as piercing sirens echo in the confined corridors. Her heart quickens, a primal instinct screaming for her to find a way out, for each breath drawn feels like borrowed time. The taste of the dusty air clings to her throat, an acrid reminder of every moment slipping dangerously away. She turns, catching Reed's gaze, both imbued with unspoken urgency, understanding the dire stakes of their predicament. Together, they move, almost in synchrony, their steps a shared pact of survival coursing through their veins.

Columns of cement stand like titans in the dim light, seedlings of doubt sprouting within her with each turn. Her mind claws at the options, the paths entangling her with memories of choices unseen, a life that never allowed this chaos a moment to settle. Each heartbeat a relentless drum, echoing through the caverns of her mind. She recognizes the outlines of an emergency exit, not by the sign but by where the air tastes of freedom, and before she knows it, she and Reed are sprinting towards it, weaving through the pandemonium, debris raining like an unyielding storm.

The corridor stretches ahead, every fiber in her urging forward; the scent of smoke is thick, almost tangible. Her muscles burn with defiance against the oppressive weight of exhaustion and fear. She senses Reed beside her, their synergy palpable, the years of fractured bonds mended here in the throes of chaos. Trust had been their tentative ally, its presence reaffirmed by the mutual reliance in each footstep echoing in the chaos. She channels her fear, a well of raw determination boiling beneath the surface as they surge through the emergency exit, the oppressive confines giving way to the blinding glare of daylight.

Yet within this liberation waits a grim greeting. Armed agents materialize like apparitions, their metal glints a silent testament to the perilous liberty now at stake. Miranda's vision narrows to the present threat, her resolve crystallizing as she navigates backward, leveraging the sun's glare to strategize her move. Her senses sharpen as Reed falters, caught in the grips of a haunting flash, his expression sliding into a realm distanced by time and trauma.

Miranda's breath falters, her fingers twitch with urgency —not with fear, but with an overwhelming need to pull them both forward. Something within her roars awake, the fight or flight instinct fueled by entwined fates as molten resolve wraps its tendrils around every heartbeat.

"Reed!" Her voice a desperate anchor.

Reality rebinds itself around him, her plea cutting through the fog of his remembrances. She meets his eyes and for a fleeting moment, all elements coalesce—past, present, fear, and trust. Reed blinks away the specters, grounding himself with the sight of her, steadied by the shared tumultuous journey that brought them here. The world seesaws back into focus as mutual recognition of their perilous stakes sharpens his gaze.

"We can't stay," Miranda calls over the din, squeezing urgency into her words. "We must keep moving!"

A nod from Reed and they're on their feet, bodies hurtling towards the unknown horizon, a pact against the abyss forged from chaos and the fragility of trust. As Miranda pulls Reed further into the maelstrom, the sun dips to cast long shadows of the agents behind them, reminders of fleeting victories and encroaching darkness. But in the thick of it, they find an unyielding determination, a tether spun from purpose and the firestorm of exposure behind them. Daylight beckons—a promise and a challenge—as they plunge into the anticipation of their next battle.

CHAPTER 11

CHASING DAYLIGHT

The Suicide Mission

Miranda and Reed step cautiously toward the imposing data center, its reflective facade gleaming under the early morning sun. The remoteness of the location amplifies the silence, each footstep amplified in the stillness as they approach the fortified entrance. Both wear drab coveralls, thick with the scent of engine oil and metal filings—perfect disguises for blending into the maintenance crew tasked with the mundane upkeep of the facility's mechanical entrails.

The air is laced with anticipation, a thick, invisible cord tightening around Miranda's chest as they pass through the sliding doors. This building holds secrets that have seeped into every corner of her existence, casting long shadows over the pieces of her past she'd rather remain hidden. As they maneuver through the labyrinth of sterile corridors, their choreography is seamless. Each movement is calculated, orchestrated to avoid the dance of the security cameras swinging lazily above their heads. The monitors buzz softly, guardians of a silence that seems to grow denser with every step she takes.

Memories of Project Morpheus flicker on the edges of her consciousness like static on an old television screen. The sheer enormity of the world's possible collapse is compressed behind the mirrored doors they pass. Miranda feels it keenly—the gravity of her decisions, her past intertwined with an operation designed to spawn chaos under the tutelage of an absent puppet master.

Soon, they arrive at the data room. Her heart thrums, synchronizing to the whirring of circuits behind thick steel. Miranda sets her toolbox down, her fingers dancing with muscle memory over the keys of her gadget. She connects the device, watching blinking lights reflect in Reed's eyes—eyes that, for all their clarity, have seen their fill of shadows.

"Focus, Reed. We've planned for this," Miranda whispers, her voice a tightly wound coil.

Reed nods, his answer a silent prayer above the humming servers, his resolve mingled with the tension of the quiet rebellion they are staging within these four walls. Overtime, the weight of what lies ahead settles over her like a second skin.

"Do you think it ever ends?" Reed breaks the tension, eyes scanning the data streams flashing across the monitor.

Miranda keeps her gaze fixed on the terminal. "If not by us, then who?"

Reed hesitates, then rips his focus back to the screen. "Yeah. You're right. It's us or no one."

The purge software activates, its rhythm a ticking metronome of digits cascading toward oblivion. They monitor the code—lines of green marching across the screen marching toward a future that, should they fail, promises to erase more than just history.

There is a tangible fragility to this moment. It feels like standing at the edge of a precipice, staring into a void where a single misstep means plummeting into chaos. Miranda inhales deeply. Here, technology becomes both sword and shield, a tangible reminder of its power to shape the world into patterns dictated by those wielding control.

A single error could unravel everything. She watches the encryption dance like the ghosts of her past, and realizes that each line erased pulls her further from the woman she was molded to be. Each keystroke echoes the sound of her freedom unfurling, thread by thread.

The computers react, their screens illuminating with measured finality. It is a moment charged with purpose. In the heart of the machine lies the last of Morpheus, and amid the sterile daemon-dance of diodes, Miranda knows she stands on the battlefield of her life—a battle where the spoils could very well define the world.

The Warden's True Nature

Alarms pierce the air, slicing through the sterile silence of the data center like a siren warning of an impending storm. Miranda stands at the terminal, her fingers dancing furiously across the keyboard. She's fueled by urgency, driven by the need to uncover whatever remnants of Project Morpheus might be buried within these digital archives. The cold glow from the screen reflects in her eyes, casting shadows that deepen the creases of tension on her face.

As she navigates the labyrinthine file system, a folder catches her eye—"The Warden: Case Studies." Her heart pounds with the weight of history as she clicks open the folder, eager to drag buried truths into the light. The air in the room seems to thicken, anticipation crackling like static electricity.

Reed edges closer, peering over her shoulder. His eyes widen as they land on the reports quickly scrolling past. The documents narrate chilling accounts of psychological manipulation, dark tales of sleeper agents wielded during the Cold War. In careful, clinical language, they describe methods of rewriting minds, of reshaping identities to suit the whims of power.

"It's all here, isn't it?" Reed's voice is low, barely audible over the mechanical hum and the cacophony blaring from the intercom. "Wars, coups... he orchestrated it all."

The depth of The Warden's machinations unfolds before them, an intricate web spun with threads of deception and control. Years of strategic interference unravel as Miranda scrolls through, each line of text a thread pulled from the fabric of modern history.

Miranda's mind is awash with conflicting emotions. She recalls the relentless pressures and promises of Project Morpheus, seductive whispers that ensnared her youth. What once seemed a noble endeavor is now exposed as a grotesque violation—bonds of trust distorted, personal agency hijacked. Memories of times past clash within her, echoes of choices that blur the lines between victimhood and complicity.

They share a moment heavy with realization. The Warden had treated the world like his chessboard, moving pawns, knights, and queens wherever they best suited his design, indifferent to the collateral damage.

Miranda's gaze meets Reed's. Without words, they affirm a shared resolve, a pledge to dismantle the remnants of this dark legacy.

The reports flash a final message across the terminal, charting a sprawling conspiracy that leaves no one untouched. It feels like standing at the heart of a storm, the truth swirling violently around them, threatening to pull everything apart. But nestled within the chaos is clarity, a beacon they cling to as they prepare to extinguish The Warden's poisonous influence once and for all.

The Network Shuts Down

Navigating the winding corridors of the high-security data center, Miranda expertly avoids security cameras with Reed at her side, every step a testament to their survival instincts honed from countless high-stakes missions. A lifetime of high-pressure scenarios sharpens her focus, memories of dangerous close calls and clever evasions playing like flickering film reels in her mind. Project Morpheus had been both her curse and her battleground, and the weight of past failures gnaws at her core, intensifying her drive to succeed swiftly and absolutely.

They reach the data room, the hum of powerful servers surrounding them as they unpack their devices with precision. The clatter of their toolboxes echoes slightly, each sound a reminder of the delicacy of their endeavor. A notification suddenly pops up—a hazardously hidden backup drive is activating, preparing to extract sensitive data. Miranda's heart pounds, the anxiety of their losing battle matching the erratic beats in her chest. Her fingers tremble slightly as she types, fearing that despite their meticulous planning, their efforts are crumbling even as they begin.

"Got to hurry," Reed mutters, his voice low, bordering on urgency. He leans over her shoulder, eyes darting between screens.

Miranda nods, her pulse racing. "If we don't stop that drive...everything's for nothing."

They scramble, fingers flying over keys in a frantic bid to overcome the system's stubborn glitch. Cold sweat forms on her brow as the screen stutters, momentarily freezing their progress. Her breaths come short and quick, a rush of desperate determination clawing at her thoughts. Boundaries between past and present blur; timelines of chaos, betrayal, and lost comrades press heavily upon her shoulders. The emotions simmer and swirl, choking her rational thought.

“It’s not responding... Reboot it manually, now!” Miranda’s voice cuts through the tension, her mind, a maelstrom of potential outcomes and the damning flutter of self-doubt. She breathes deep, drawing strength from the memory of every obstacle she has surmounted before.

The system kicks back to life with a whir, and within seconds, they execute the destroy command—but only for the main servers. Relief is fleeting. Each flash on the screen is a reminder of the pieces cascading beyond their reach, shadowed whispers threatening from behind her defiant streak.

"What about the backup?" Reed asks, the air thickening as distant shouts grow louder, footsteps echoing menacingly down the corridors they just crept through.

Miranda locks eyes with him, a fraction of dread creeping beneath her calm façade. They exchange a silent, loaded look, acknowledging the stakes; nothing has ever felt quite so personal or so perilous.

"Can't leave it." Her voice firm, she banishes every lurking fear to the shadowed corners of her mind. "We pursue it. Disable the drive if we can. Or stop the physical transfer altogether." The declaration solidifies in the crisp air around them, a rallying cry amidst the encroaching storm. The realization sharpens—waiting is no option, not when threads of her past and strands of possible futures tangle together with such desperation.

Reed nods once, quick and resolute, as the guard shouts beat like a war drum, encircling them. Their decision etched in fleeting glances, they ready themselves for the impending torrent, and with bated breath, dive deeper into the heart of uncertainty.

The Warden's Escape

Shadows drape the corridor as an ominous voice echoes through the facility's intercom. "You cannot erase what is already inside you," it declares, chilling Miranda to the core. Her heart pounds as the realization settles like lead in her stomach, each word gnawing at her resolve. Her breath catches, and she feels the all-too-familiar grip of Project Morpheus tightening around the frayed edges of her psyche.

The message reverberates through her mind, dredging up memories she had hoped were buried for good. Images, fleeting and fragmented, flash behind her eyes—cold clinical rooms, whispered commands, her own reflection staring back at her with hollow eyes. She yearns to push them away, but they cling, relentless and suffocating, sowing seeds of doubt and fear.

Her gaze shifts to Reed, his presence a beacon in the swirling chaos. He reads the unease etched on her face and steps closer, his voice firm yet laced with concern. "Don't let it get to you, Miranda. We need to stay focused."

His words attempt to cut through the fog of dread enveloping her. She clutches onto his presence like a lifeline, knowing that staying grounded is imperative. There is a genuine, albeit fragile, alliance between them, one born out of shared peril and necessity. In this moment of tension, he becomes an anchor, tethering her to the mission at hand rather than the shadows of her past.

"I won't let him control us anymore," Miranda vows, her voice filled with a resolve she wills herself to believe. The specter of The Warden looms large, casting a pall over their determination, but she harnesses the fear coursing through her into something akin to courage.

A smirk flickers briefly across Reed's face, and in it, Miranda finds a glimmer of mutual understanding. Despite the chaos, this moment cements their bond, a silent promise that they will stand together against the looming threat of The Warden's manipulations. Together, they steel themselves, drawing strength from the shared commitment to defy the tangles of their past.

In the distance, alarms scream an urgent symphony. Their shared resolve wraps around them like armor as Miranda takes a steadying breath. They are not alone, not totally fractured, and as they prepare to fight back, the weight of The Warden's influence remains daunting yet defiable. With Reed at her side, Miranda's fear transmutes into fierce determination, ready to combat the insidious shadow threatening to consume her world.

The System Burns

The facility lurches violently as if it is a living entity under siege, shaking the very foundation beneath their feet. Reed's muscles tighten as he feels the unpredictability in the air, an electrical charge crackling from the alarms wailing their persistent warning. Miranda positions herself beside him, cast in the cold artificial glow of flickering lights, her steady breathing a rhythmic anchor amidst the chaos. They scurry forward, instinctively synchronizing their steps down the dimly lit corridors, dodging a barrage of shattered ceiling tiles and the panicked exodus of their fellow escapees--staff, once anonymous, now desperate figures in a shared flight.

Their path narrows into a bottleneck of humanity—a chaotic congregation jostling for the narrow promise of safety, guarded by uniformed sentinels. The guards, a wall of implacability, demand identification and exclamations of betrayal echo in the labyrinth. The collective panic is a crescendo that threatens to swallow them whole. Reed's mind sifts through his mental atlas of the facility, scrutinizing every unworn crease for a way out.

"Vent shaft, over there," Miranda's voice steers him away from the precipice of indecision. Her index finger points true, guiding them toward the forgotten exit lying beyond conventional egress. The revelation casts a stark contrast between confidence and doubt, but Reed nods, drawing strength from her resolve.

Agility replaces fear as they maneuver toward the escape route, contorting delicately into the vent's metallic maw. Cold, stale air rushes past them, intensifying Reed's senses, eclipsed only by the metallic tang clinging to his taste buds. Familiarity offers no comfort; every inch of the shaft feels like uncharted peril as elbows and knees propel them forward in a cramped dance of survival. Metallic clangs pulse in harmony with the facility's heartbeat, each clang a reminder of impending collapse behind them.

Their bodies spill out onto the world's edge, the raw kiss of mountain air filling their lungs like a promise of freedom. It tastes of pine and ice—freedom's bittersweet elixir. Staggered, they rise in unison against the majestic violence of the Alps, the narrative of the battle behind painting a question mark upon their futures.

Reed's eyes trace a path back over their shoulder, over the smoldering silhouette of the collapsing monument to cruelty. Their ordeal rumbles into memory—the juddering end of one phase and the uncertainty of what lies ahead. Peculiar emotions churn within as he studies the remnants of their past struggles--unsure but resolute.

Through the grey mist of fatigue, a looming determination kindles within Reed. The echoes of previous battles swirl within him, an urgent reminder that the fight against The Warden's shadow ensures no respite. It seeps into his bones, fragments of duty and doubt twining tighter with each breath, urging him onward into the unknown abyss of whatever destiny waits.

The Final Setup

Adrenaline courses through Miranda's veins as she and Reed huddle together at a safe distance from the crumbling facility. Dust hangs thick in the air, and the distant wail of sirens creates a dissonant backdrop. Hands trembling, Miranda retrieves her secure phone, the bright glow cutting through the half-light. A notification flashes, demanding her attention. She hesitates before tapping to reveal the message, aware that whatever awaits could change everything.

Her heart sinks as she scans the details: a new wave of Morpheus activation is set to trigger the next day. Each chilling detail carves deeper lines of worry into her face. Sleepers embedded in positions of power, waiting like loaded guns across the globe. Terror sneaks under her skin—how many more have yet to awake, puppets to The Warden's final note?

The air smells of smoke and fear as she turns to Reed, her voice a rushed whisper. "We're not done yet. The activation is still rolling forward. Tomorrow. More sleeper agents are on standby for activation. It's all set to amplify the chaos."

Reed processes her words in stunned silence, his shoulders sagging under the weight of the revelation. His features, usually a stoic mask, falter.

Miranda studies him, waiting for the spark of resolve she knows he possesses. "I know it seems insurmountable, but we can't let this happen. We've come too far."

His eyes meet hers, tinged with shared desperation, and something else—determination. Silence speaks volumes as they prepare for the battles that lie ahead, knowing that the threads of their lives are now inextricably tied to this struggle.

Miranda's mind races, considering the societal chasm Project Morpheus has split open, devouring trust in institutions, fracturing the fragile weave of global peace. The depth of The Warden's conspiracy is staggering, infiltrating the bones of power structures built to protect society. Yet, in a world shrouded in shadows of deceit, she realizes they now embody a fragile hope against the encroaching darkness.

Her pulse steadies, grounding her somewhere between terror and steel-willed determination. Racing thoughts shift to the looming possibility of erasure—a clean slate, free from the chains that bind her past. Could she ever break free from the specter of The Warden's commands, the tendrils of programming woven into the fabric of who she is? The prospect is both inviting and suffocating. Self-obliteration wraps around her heart like a serpent, whispering promises of peace, yet a pernicious fear lingers—what if part of her identity was abandoned to the void?

She shakes off the notion, choosing to cleave to the strength buried beneath the trauma. Project Morpheus will not define her future. Whatever shadows it casts upon her soul, she will navigate them, carving a path forward through the truth she unravels and the lies she dismantles.

Reed's voice pierces her resolve, calling her back to the present. "We don’t back down. We can find them. We have to—before they destroy everything."

Their eyes lock, an unspoken bond forged in the crucible of shared purpose. Miranda nods, conviction lighting a fire in her chest. The message on her screen may signal impending catastrophe, but it also galvanizes her resolve. Together, they will uproot The Warden's poisonous legacy, whatever the cost. Shoulder to shoulder with Reed, she braces for the fight to come, stepping into the dusk of uncertainty with unyielding resolve wrapped around her like armor.

CHAPTER 12

THE LAST DECEPTION

Revelations in the Digital Shadows

In the dim, cluttered space of her office, the only light emanates from the computer screen, casting a ghostly glow across Miranda Carter's focused face. The hours have stretched longer than anticipated, the night threatening to dissolve into morning, yet here they are—leaning forward into the bluish radiation of damning footage. It plays in a loop: the Morpheus operative moving through a city street with eerie precision, a crime unfurling amidst unsuspecting pedestrians who remain blissfully oblivious to the darkness shadowing their steps.

Miranda scrutinizes every detail, her eyes flitting across the various angles captured by multiple surveillance cameras. Her heart echoes the rhythmic click of a clock nearby, each second a reminder that time is slipping through their fingers. Beside her, Reed taps a pen anxiously, brows drawn as the fragmentary video remains stubbornly silent about its secrets.

Her mind drifts involuntarily, back to the inception of Project Morpheus: an unassuming sleep therapy initiative that spiraled into something far more insidious. Government-sanctioned safeguards melted away, leaving unchecked power in the hands of those who saw human minds as malleable clay. Miranda remembers how the project's promises once intrigued her, the thought of healing sleep disorders overshadowing the ethical chasm it dangerously skirted. Now, she watches the dehumanizing aftermath, grappled with the dark truth of sleeper agents saturating society—agents she once unwittingly helped to create.

"Do you see it?" Reed's voice cuts through the fog of recollection, banishing the specters of memory. His question hangs heavy between them, like a nebulous cloud of dread waiting to descend.

"I do," she responds, forced to confront the unmistakable pattern emerging from the chaos: Morpheus agents, not dormant, but distinctly active. Her thoughts ricochet between disbelief and an escalating sense of duty, acutely aware that society views her as both protector and potential threat.

"The scope," Reed begins, struggling to put his apprehension into words, "is so much larger than we thought. If they're reactivating agents like this..."

Miranda rubs her forehead, attempting to smooth out the tension threatening to crack her façade. "And the more we dig, the more tangled we become in it."

Reed mutters something under his breath—half prayer, half expletive. Miranda chooses not to press for clarity, understanding too well the weight carried in their shared silences. They are bound by necessity now, a fragile alliance poised on the edge of a knife, both questioning how long they can maintain balance.

Amidst their sifting through reports, a sudden notification pings on Miranda's computer, disrupting the room's solemn quietude. An encrypted message flashes across the screen, urgent and dire: a new activation sequence is imminent within the next 24 hours. The magnitude of the implication strikes her with paralyzing clarity. Her breath catches, driven by the realization that the darkness is gaining ground faster than they've managed to stem its advance.

Miranda's focus narrows, attention transfixed by the illuminated text as her mind races ahead to weigh potential counteractions against the unveiled threat. The grim clarity of her task is reflected in the simmering determination that hardens her resolve; she knows she cannot allow the specter of Morpheus to eclipse everything they've fought so hard to dismantle.

She stares silently at the monitor, absorbing the gravity of their newfound knowledge. The room's silence reverberates with the palpable risk they now face. Each second seems to pulse with the agonizing pace of inevitability, leaving Miranda burdened with the role she's played and the complex web of secrets still waiting to ensnare them all.

The Ultimatum Chamber

Miranda Carter stands in a cold, unforgiving government conference room, her eyes tracing the impassive faces gathered around the long, smooth table. The space is sterile; its walls, a clinical shade of white, are devoid of any warmth or familiarity, exuding an atmosphere that's as reassuring as a surgical knife. A large digital screen hangs at one end, silently forecasting the scope of the new phase of Morpheus with infinite precision and indifference.

The officials murmur, their voices as measured as their tailored suits, and lay bare the unsettling breadth of the Morpheus project's next steps. Every word is a calculated maneuver, a silent dance of authority and persuasion. Miranda sits rigidly, knowing the weight she carries—this is not a conversation about abstract political games; this is her life, her morality, her soul splayed open on this cold, Venetian table.

As they offer her the chance to fall back into the role of operative, a shadow from her past brushes against her, colder than the room itself. The air grows thick with unspoken consequences, and Miranda can almost feel the fibers of indecision winding around her chest. She remembers the unfamiliar sense of power and purpose that came with being an agent, yet she's haunted by the loss of autonomy it demanded. This isn't just about her; her decision could shape the invisible boundaries that bind others in ways they cannot perceive.

Her perception of herself floats like a leaf on a torrent of conflicting truths and half-remembered directives, remnants of The Warden's whispering legacy. She debates silently, weighing the iron grip of the past against the tangible possibilities of the present. Reinstatement means safety from the slow, dark crawl of imprisonment, but it also means blinding herself willingly to the moral chasm onto which Morpheus was built. Her fingers drum an uneven rhythm against the table, the echoes of her turmoil.

"Rejoining risks everything," Miranda argues, her voice level but edged with fatigue. "It means perpetuating this cycle of control, weaving deeper into these systems that profit off deception and fear." She looks into the eyes of one of the officials, daring to challenge the façade of order they uphold. "The ethical cost here isn't one I'm ready to shoulder—a margin of error involving lives." Her heart pounds—a rebellious cadence against the inevitabilities that the world seeks to leash her with.

The officials, unflinching, press forward like assured predators. Their ultimatum crashes over her like a cold wave, a choice carved from stark necessity: reintegrate and play their sacrificial pawn, or resist and face the chasm of consequences alone. Her defenses build up, an instinctual fortress around her soul, now alert and watchful.

She stands silent, her eyes skating the room—familiar faces turned foreign by the demand for allegiance. They remain impassive, the chorus of her unsaid thoughts echoing in the tiny crackles of static from the speakers. Miranda's mind spins corridors of recollection, expanding into vistas of veiled manipulation and engineered loyalty—this hidden machinery of state that neither softens nor gives.

The government's history with psychological programs like Morpheus is a shadow dimension where fear prospers and manipulations loom like obelisks over the truth tellers. It was an intricate web, spun in secrecy, cloaked in deception, threading itself into the unsuspecting fabric of society. The climate of control and regulation seeped into reality, breeding a world where doubt thrives on control.

Miranda breathes deeply, absorbing the room's chill, her thoughts untethering into a dissonance of dread and resolve. The stakes loom at the periphery—her acquiescence could mean repentance or betrayal, her defiance, liberation or demise. In this systemic whirlpool of deceit, could she ever emerge unscathed, free, absolved in her own eyes?

The moment stretches out before her. She holds her choice, a palpable, feather-light weight, hearing only the soft murmur of her conscience and the thrill of anticipation. The sound of her heart gives a formless rhythm to the cacophony within. She stands, expression unreadable, a storm of decisions locked tight against stillness, standing at the cusp of a world, whether forsaken or unredeemed.

Silence envelops the room; Miranda stands still, contemplating the government's ultimatum, feeling its weight press against her soul, trembling at the edge of refraction.

Ghosts of Control

In the dim glow of her apartment, Miranda Carter sits hunched over a cluttered desk, shadows of past choices crowding around like unwelcome ghosts. Flickering lamplight dances over the worn edges of old case files and photographs, the memories they hold as vivid and intrusive as reminiscing spirits. Each file she opens is a window into a time when Project Morpheus dictated the music to which she danced—a time that masqueraded as freedom, while in truth, she was tethered to invisible strings.

Her fingers graze over a photograph, the glossy finish cold under her touch. Smiling faces smile back, oblivious to the invisible chains that bind them. Behind that smile, the true visage of The Warden lurks—a man whose whispers wove tales of control disguised as liberation. She had believed in those tales once, believed in the notion that she was a maestro of her fate, not realizing she was merely a pawn on his expansive chessboard. The echo of his voice, persuasive and insidious, reverberates in her mind, questioning her autonomy, her very essence. Could she ever truly break free from the iron grips of her past, or were these scars embedded too deeply into her soul?

Miranda envisions vivid moments, pivotal conversations that were once nothing but moments but are now mountains, casting long shadows over her psyche. The Warden had a predilection for probing words, ones that seeped into her thoughts like a noxious gas, suffocating her sense of self. As she sifts through these fragments, her decisions weigh heavily, leaving impressions on her conscience that make her skin crawl. It's a familiar prison —a conflict between her yearning for escape and the guilt burdening her shoulders like lead weights.

Despite the cacophony of thoughts raging within, a seed of resolve takes root among the ruins of past despair. She knows she cannot allow the specter of Morpheus to victimize another. The stakes stretch beyond her solitude, beyond her memories, reaching into the fabric of the lives of countless innocents. Pacing, she closes the last file; determination etches itself into her features. The past can't be altered, but its echo need not dictate her future. She can and will carve out a path, even if it means forging through the fire anew, at any cost. Miranda Carter is ready.

Storms of Defiance

The storm rages outside, wind howling like a restless spirit as lightning splits the sky, briefly illuminating the confines of Miranda's apartment. Each flash is a stark reminder of the tempest churning within her. Her gaze sits heavy on the window, lost in contemplation amidst the symphony of rain drumming against the panes.

Her phone buzzes on the table, cutting through the storm's wail. The glow of the screen seems to pulse in the darkness, and with a reluctant hand, she reaches for it. The message is short, cryptic—a fresh cut on a scarred psyche: “You’ve only seen the first layer of this.”

The words set her heart racing. Her mind wrestles with the implications, the depth of The Warden’s web unfathomable as it sprawls across her thoughts. What if The Warden's reach is as infinite as the stormy sky above, each raindrop a sleeper agent waiting for the signal? What if she's been a pawn in his game all along—or worse, an unwitting antagonist, another layer to peel away?

Miranda stands at the precipice of her own fears, each new thought like thunder reverberating through her mind. Each "what if" weaves a tighter cocoon around her, leaving her breathless with the weight of possibilities. Could she become another weapon, another mask of agency ready to crumble under The Warden's gaze? These questions haunt her, an insidious whisper that never fades.

Her fingers dance over the phone, poised between action and paralysis. The message may have been concise, but its brevity is a beacon of dread, leading her through dark corridors of conjecture she fears to traverse. She clenches her jaw, molding her anxiety into something formidable. A resolution—as stark, as vivid as the streaks of light tearing the night—takes hold. She has waded through too much blood, felt the weight of too many ghosts. If The Warden is still out there pulling strings, she'll sever them herself.

Lightning crashes again, outlining the resolve etched into her features. The storm is inside and out—her heart mirrored by the tempest. The phone clicks off with finality, captured in her tightening grasp. She isn't captive to fear any longer; she is a hunter against the unknown layers The Warden hides behind.

Clarity comes in fleeting moments, like lightning amidst the clouds. She must act, must pull at these threads until the tapestry of control unravels. The phone, her lifeline and noose, comes alive one more time. A promise unwritten, to find every last sleeper under The Warden's thrall and cast them into the light. Miranda's jaw is set, her heart a drumbeat of determination. She has decided —freedom is a battle yet to be fought, and she's only just begun.

Dawn of Reckoning

Miranda stands amid the scattered remnants of her past, a fortitude of unsorted files and scattered photographs detailing months of teasing out threads from the tangled skein of Project Morpheus. As dawn edges over the horizon, the first rays of light fracture the gloom in her apartment, laying bare a landscape cluttered with documents and the lethality of weaponry—a calculated arsenal prepped for whatever may come.

Breath held in the throes of introspection, Miranda drags a palm over her brow, the tactile reminder grounding her. Could she erase her past as easily as wiping clean a slate, or was she merely inviting a new shade of control to clasp her chains? The specter of past manipulations claws at her, questioning whether freedom found through forgetfulness would last, or merely herald a subtler cage. The very thought is suffocating, like waves pulling her under only for her to break surface at the last moment, gasping. Could she ever truly fathom the depths to which she had sunk and risen again? Or was she doomed to forever revisit this cycle, caught in the undertow of memory?

Reed's arrival shatters the quiet. He stands at the door, the creak of his shadow a prelude to the weight of his words. His gaze wavers between the array of arms and stacks of papers marking Miranda's renewed commitment to the cause. His voice, accompanied by the rustle of morning light, dances around uncertainties.

"Do we even know how deep this goes, or are we gambling blind?" His question lingers, infused with weary resolve, reinforcing the chasm of doubt.

"We've come too far to turn back," Miranda responds, her voice a whisper of grit. "If we retreat now, we surrender everything we've fought for."

There's a flicker of hesitation, Reed's shoulders heavy with shadows of an unnamable burden—one that Miranda knows all too well. His once-clear lines of loyalty now frayed, memories pocked with moments administered under Morpheus's guise.

They dissect intel and finalize their strategy, their dialogue an exchange forged in equal parts trust and trepidation. Should Reed's control waver under triggers unseen, what then? The enormity of relying on him sends a ripple through her confidence, dragging specters of doubt in its wake. But still, there's faith—a tenuous thread connecting them, one stronger than her tremors of anxiety.

"You're sure you're ready for this?" Reed's words turn the space brittle, the resonance of unasked doubts coloring the air.

"We don't have a choice, Reed. It's us or them."

The intensity of their shared mission looms among the shadows, binding their resolve in knots shaped by adversity. What once lay buried now finds wings beneath it—a dawning awareness of shared purpose shaped against the specter of Morpheus.

As dawn unfurls beyond the narrow confines of her apartment, Miranda pushes open the door, the creak akin to unfurling an unwritten future. She and Reed exchange a glance, a silent pact formed from the ash of past betrayals and shared burdens.

They step out into the emerging haze of day. The air is laden with promise, swirling about them in a vortex of hope tempered by resolve. Miranda's steps are steadier than before, her breath a determined whisper against the fate that clings stubbornly to her shadow. Together, they walk into the early dawn, their silhouettes fading into the horizon, set ablaze by intentions clear and path uncertain.

CHAPTER 13

THE FALL OF THE WARDEN

Silent Convergence Under Alpine Stars

Under the star-studded canopy of the Swiss Alps, Miranda and Reed crouch behind a boulder, their breaths mingling with the crisp night air. The forest hum surrounds them—unseen creatures rustling in the underbrush, the whispers of an alpine breeze. Miranda clutches the edges of her stealth suit, adjusting it for warmth as she narrows her eyes toward the outline of the underground facility ahead, nothing but a shadow against the starlit sky. The mission encases her thoughts like iron, each step a crucial move in dismantling Project Morpheus, a machine of global subversion she was once unwittingly a part of.

The sound of night envelops them as they creep through the underbrush, thoughts threading through Miranda's mind more frenetic than the careful placement of her steps. The covert world they have stepped into doesn't forgive missteps; every decision counts, lives poised like dominoes on her choices. As they move, the contours of past betrayals and lost fragments of her previous life within Morpheus flash like lightning through her conscience—a gauntlet of memories she'd rather leave shadowed in the depths. The stakes pressed against her chest feel immense, yet the determination running through her is unyielding.

Reed sidles close behind a terminal and, despite the palpable threat lurking in the silence, can't help but comment. “We’re threading a pretty tight needle here,” he whispers, his voice low, enveloped in the dense undergrowth.

Miranda nods, her gaze firm and acknowledging. “This ends tonight,” she replies, the words catching a touch in the still air, an affirmation to both him and herself. The stakes thrum beneath her skin—the sprawling potential of Morpheus continuing unimpeded, a specter dangling over international stability and safety. Governments and shadowed alliances gleam with culpability, in thrall to a culture that bends morality for the façade of control.

Silent as phantoms, they approach a heavy metal door marked “Security Access Only.” Reed, tools in hand, makes the lockpicking appear as art, each click and shift a promise that they won’t be stopped today. Miranda stands guard, attuned to every shiver of sound in the encroaching darkness, broadening her focus from her own haunting vulnerabilities to encompass the lives entwined in this web of secrecy. The program’s revival spells more than a loss of identity; it threatens the existence of those unseen, the world beneath the reality to which most remain blissfully ignorant.

Inside the main control room, they find themselves swallowed by an array of illuminated screens, glowering with maps that punctuate the room in pulsing red lights. Each pinpoint a testament to Morpheus’ reach, sleeper agents poised like marionettes weighted by strings. The floor beneath them seems to ripple with a hum from the systems, resonating with the intricacies of manipulation far beyond the room's boundaries.

Their eyes meet across the blue-lit console, both digesting the immediate imperative. In that shared glance lies an understanding—this moment could carve the course of countless lives. Miranda's resolve hardens, forged in the crucible of fear and the promise of redemption. The price of her past may never truly settle, but right now, her path lies unmasked before her—a chance to reclaim autonomy not just for herself, but for all those tethered by invisible cords. With a deep breath, they draw strength from shared silence, steeling themselves for what lies ahead.

Fractured Allegiance

The control room's sterile calm fills the underground facility, the soft thrum of machinery a backdrop to the flickering glow of screens lining the walls. Suddenly, the speakers crackle, filling the room with a booming, omnipresent voice. It's The Warden, authoritative and commanding, and his revelation pierces through the tense air like a knife. "Activate Command Sequence: Omega," he declares, and those words unravel everything.

Reed's posture shifts, his shoulders locking in place as if a puppet on strings. The change in him is like a shadow passing over a once-familiar landscape, leaving only rigidity and the harsh edge of control. Gone is the warmth and humanity that Miranda knows so well; it's replaced with something machine-like, something terrifyingly other.

He turns, not with the gentle gaze of an ally but with eyes that blaze with an artificial fire. His movements are jerky, staccato, as if resistance holds every muscle taut. His face is a mask, showing none of the turmoil that she can only guess eats at him inside. Miranda's heart aches with a confused cocktail of betrayal and empathy.

As he advances, the mechanical determination in his steps cuts through the room's stillness. She braces herself, instincts honed by countless trials kicking in. Her mind races—she knows success depends on reaching the Reed who exists beneath the surface programming, the Reed who has fought alongside her against a tide of darkness.

"Reed!" Miranda calls out, slipping easily into a defensive stance. The world narrows to the immediate, every sense honed to the actions and decisions of this uncertain confrontation. "It's me. Remember what we're fighting for!"

Her voice echoes, steady and unwavering, slicing through the heavy fog of dominance The Warden tries to impose. She pivots, dodging a rush that carries an unsettling mixture of familiarity and force. As blows come, the choreography of combat becomes a dance infused with meaning beyond mere survival—the dance of their partnership unfolding under the threat of annihilation.

"You're stronger than this. We both are!" Miranda insists, her voice threading through the chaos, reaching for the depth beyond his current state. Her defense isn't just physical; it's a heartfelt plea to break through the layers of hidden commands and buried truths. Each word she utters is like a key, turning against the locks The Warden cruelly placed.

Reed pauses, his fist inches from its mark, hovering between the mechanical and the human. She can see hesitation reflecting in his features, a brief flicker of the man who shares memories, battles, laughter, and despair.

"Remember," she says softly now, shunning anger for kinship. "Remember who you truly are."

Confusion etches itself across his face, a war between the command to destroy and the history they've forged together. Miranda holds her ground, embodying an unspoken promise not to yield, not to lose faith. As she witnesses the internal shift, as if a shroud lifts within his eyes, she knows the battle for identity rages within but remains winnable.

Slowly, the hand poised in aggression lowers, a tremor of uncertainty vibrating through its descent. In that delicate moment of silence—and vulnerability—she sees Reed emerge, searching, rediscovering, his aggression softening into something lived and known.

Fragments of Redemption

The aftermath of Reed's attack ripples across the control room, an uneasy quiet settling over the screens that still pulse with global maps of sleeper agents. Miranda inches closer, her eyes fixed on Reed, whose posture is now rigid, his fists still drawn in surrender to forces he can't see but Miranda knows too well. She leans in, her voice a whisper barely slicing the charged air.

"Remember, Reed. You're more than this," she murmurs, invoking a counter-trigger rooted deeply within his subconscious, a phrase embedded in their past to pull him back from the brink. Her whisper is like a lifeline tethered to reality, pulling him from the depths of a nightmare.

Reed's expression falters, blank for seconds stretched thin by anticipation. His muscles, taut with the pull of conflicting commands, start to ease. The glint of fervor in his eyes wavers, replaced by the faint glow of recognition. His hands unclench, dropping limply to his sides like marionette strings cut by force of will.

He inhales sharply, the ragged breath of a man emerging from beneath heavy waters, each exhalation carrying fragments of lost memories and convictions painstakingly reconstructed. The room bears silent witness to Reed's reclamation of self—a battleground now hushed with the weight of personal victory. He collapses to the floor, his bulky form consumed with the agitated shiver of release.

Miranda kneels beside him, placing a firm hand on his shoulder—an anchor in the storm of his unrelenting doubt. She spins the tapestry of her quiet reassurance, threading through the fractures in his psyche with measured patience. Her belief that he is a fighter, armed against injustice rather than complicit in it, infuses the space, cushioning the jagged edges of their shared ordeal.

This very room, thrumming with the residual hum of disrupted systems, bears witness not only to Reed's collapse but to their united strength. A strength drawn from every moment abandoned to old orders now unraveled—manifold threads of trained instincts interwoven with spurred growth. And as silence spreads its mantle, Miranda and Reed rise, their resolve a bulwark against the lingering chaos, eyes set upon the shadowed door that births new trials.

Ultimatum of Shadows

The control room's lights flicker, casting twisted shadows across the cold steel walls before stabilizing, and in the sterile fluorescence, The Warden steps forward. His presence is a shadow that fills the room, the embodiment of manipulation and control, his eyes holding an unsettling calm. He carries an air of quiet authority, aged with the wisdom of a man who has spent years navigating the murky waters of political machination.

Miranda stands opposite him, a figure wrapped in defiance. Her voice, though steady, cuts through the space between them with a sharpness honed by resolve. Reed, barely recovering his sense of self, leans against the console; his presence a testament to their shared struggles and triumphs. The Warden's voice, as smooth as it is powerful, weaves a narrative of grand design—a new world order, meticulously crafted for what he perceives as the greater good.

Once, nations wrestled in open conflict in a theater of brutality, but now, The Warden claims, subtler measures are needed. In his eyes, Project Morpheus is a necessary evolution. It is a tool, an improvement upon the blunt instruments of old, crafted to fit a world teetering on the brink of chaos. He sees his sleeper agents as guardians of stability, essential warriors in a silent war over humanity's soul. For him, the morality of such actions are easily justified with historic parallels; nations have always pursued power through more insidious means, and he is merely refining the approach.

"You're blind if you think this is any different from the tyranny you claim to prevent," Miranda retorts, her words coming quick and hot, fueled by indignation. "Free will isn't a pawn to be sacrificed. It's the foundation of everything we stand for."

The Warden exhales, a wry smile etching the lines of a face accustomed to control. "You see chaos, Dr. Carter, but what I offer is order. In the complex dance of power, one must sometimes guide the feet of those who falter."

“There’s no guiding here,” Miranda counters sharply, each word a precise incision against the veil of The Warden's justifications. “Only binding chains, only the deceit that serves your interests. We won’t be your tools."

In The Warden's conviction lies a belief that stability trumps the anarchy of choice. He views her not as a rival but as a misguided prophet, preaching freedom in a world that, to him, needs firm hands on the reins. Internally, he reasons that a few individuals must surely suffer to shield many from suffering. It is a balancing act of necessity, he justifies, an orchestration of events to usher in a utopia untainted by the volatility of unchecked humanity.

Reed’s confusion begins to dissolve, knowing full well the allure of simplicity in The Warden’s worldview. Yet, his instincts warn of deeper corruption beneath the veneer of benevolence that The Warden wraps himself in. The room’s tension swells as each breath seems to carry the weight of unfinished battles and unspoken fears. With Miranda at his side, he finds clarity, an awakening that galvanizes their resistance.

As Miranda stands unwavering, her defiance a banner against the unnatural quiet of the room, Reed follows. Their shared look is a silent promise to stand resolute against the false order, determined to shatter the illusion of control, aware of the risks but ready to forge a path through the chaos. Their decision made, they prepare for the turn that must come, the battle against The Warden's darkness looming close, shadows encircling the room like ghosts of power unspent.

Countdown to Liberation

Miranda's heart pounds with a rhythm as relentless as the echoing alarms that fill the room. Her fingers fly over the keys, a dance imbued with urgency and purpose. With every keystroke, she reaches deeper into the command console, drawing forth the virus that will sever the lifeline sustaining Project Morpheus. The control room, bathed in an ominous crimson glow, pulses around her with danger.

Ahead of her, The Warden stands like an imposing shadow, his mask of composure cracking. His voice, once smooth and condescending, now carries a harsh edge. "You'll never make it in time," he snarls, threats masquerading as prophecies. Miranda doesn't respond to him; her determination fuels her resolve, a wildfire he cannot quench.

Close by, Reed stands vigilant, each movement precise, as if drawing strength from Miranda's unwavering focus. Guards storm toward them, but his vigilance is unyielding. Bullets ricochet, clinking against cold steel in a deadly symphony. Yet Miranda knows he stands as her bulwark, a pillar holding up the fragile hopes they cling to.

The console's display flashes—a countdown clock begins its descent. Seconds bleed into an all-consuming rush that grips her, time slipping like sand through her fingers. She catches a breath, steadying herself against panic's cloying grasp. What happens when this countdown reaches zero? Will the world outside these walls shift, shedding its layers of control and menace, or will it simply rearrange its chains?

Somewhere, beneath the fury of alarms and gunfire, she remembers those who languished under Morpheus's grip. Lives twisted and commandeered by unseen strings. Was this her life's culmination? A strange clarity settles over her, the realization that this fight defines more than her survival—it defines her humanity.

As moments extinguish, Miranda remains rooted, her spirit unmoving. Reed fights on, empowered by the unspoken promise that this ends today. Holding tight to the knowledge that darkness neither accepts nor forgives, Miranda focuses, ready to embrace whatever dawn may come. Piece by piece, they dismantle what was built on the bones of freedom, rewriting a future with each second that ticks by fervently.

The virus races through systems, gnarling its way to the core of the network; each deletion feels like the relief of unshed tears. Amidst the chaos, Miranda glimpses that fragile flicker of hope—the universe is malleable, bendable to the desires of those resolute enough to try. She will not be shaped by its darkness any longer. As the room pulsates with impending closure, she knows they are on the precipice of more than just survival—they are on the brink of deliverance.

Emergence from the Abyss

Concrete walls vibrate as the bunker shakes violently, plunging the room into sporadic darkness when the alarms blare overhead. The Warden has activated his failsafe—a desperate blackout spreading like wildfire across the globe. Reed, with his jaw tightly clenched, adjusts his grip on Miranda's arm as chaos escalates around them. Communications buzz urgently, their frantic alerts filling the growing void of sound and sight as systems begin to fail.

Grabbing their essentials, Miranda's eyes flick to Reed. They share a silent understanding, a language spoken through shared battles and trust forged in trials. The bunker's corridors stretch out like veins trembling under seismic tremors, every echo a reminder of what's at stake—repression to freedom, shadow to light. Reed retracts his senses inward, feeling the weight of history weigh down heavier than the gear slung over his shoulder.

The corridor narrows, debris scattering across the concrete like autumn leaves. Each step, a sweep of synchrony between Reed and Miranda, is measured, deliberate, a dance of survival among the shuddering halls. Memories chase them—the twisted origins of Project Morpheus, the unethical experiments seeded by The Warden's hands. Reed's mind races; once, the directives of those experiments felt remote, just whispers among missions and cut-short conversations. Now, they are tethered to his very essence, spinning life into a web entwined with duplicity and peril.

His thoughts swirl like fragments of torn fabric. Miranda's silhouette leads them through this hive of darkness, her determination his compass. She is the voice that spoke of resilience, a voice that echoes beyond the pragmatic battles into the depths of Reed's psyche. Buried under layers of past and purpose, a part of him stirs—fighting against the programmed instinct that once would've obliterated this mission.

Caught by the tumultuous atmosphere, Reed is transported back for a cruel instant—flashes of times gone, sketched into the somber recesses of his mind. Faces of those before him, pawns to a cause they never chose, victims to the schematics of war built with blind obedience and silence. Reed wonders about their forgotten stories, those half-lived lives reprogrammed into subsistence for something that cared little for life.

Their path narrows as they near the exit. Personnel stagger past them, disoriented and fraying at the seams of confusion and fear. It's the same kind of chaos that filled Reed's chest when Miranda whispered what only they shared—those hidden words that reignite a conscience misplaced and found again. With every step in the shadowy corridors and slipping past those they cannot save, Reed's instincts sharpen, tethered to a truth shared and embraced.

They break the surface, then—bursting from the malfunctioning bunker. Their feet hit the cold earth, faces bitten by the icy breath of the Alps, under a canopy of stars. The world beyond stretches vast, an expanse free of shadows that lingered too long beneath the surface. In the rawness of this open space, Reed stands beside

Miranda, the trials behind them laboriously transformed into something new ahead—a gamut of alliance and echo, of healing and continuation.

They glance at one another, words unnecessary, their bond sealed through turmoil and redemption. The landscape ahead both holds secrets still to be uncovered and the promise of a future redefined. Together, they have stepped from darkness into a world altered not merely by events they defied, but by the strength drawn from what once was.

CHAPTER 14

THE AFTERMATH OF HORROR

Shadows on the Alpine Edge

The rumble of the collapsing fortress recedes as Miranda and Reed stagger into the icy embrace of the Swiss Alps, their breaths ragged from the sprint through chaos. Snowflakes descend lazily, a stark juxtaposition to the tumult they've escaped. The crisp air fills Reed's lungs, sharp and bracing, a reminder of life continuing beyond the havoc. They stand on the edge of a precipice, their shadows stretched long and somber against the snow—a landscape undisturbed by the violence they've unleashed.

Reed turns back, eyes tracing the path of destruction they've left. The fortress, now a mere shadow of secrecy broken and battered, haunts him. Each creak and groan of its falling beams echo with phantoms of his own past, his own hands—unwitting, he tells himself—dripping with guilt. He feels like a marionette who's just severed his strings, but what if he was never the puppeteer? What if he was the hand guiding the blade, his own hand, stained and trembling?

The scene behind is surreal, almost theatrical in its catastrophe, and Reed's thoughts tumble, lurching in refusal to comprehend. He thinks of the promises he made—to serve, to protect—and the bodies, faceless now, that litter his memories, their weight a millstone around his neck. Questions batter his mind: What am I now? Did those duties morph into crimes when I wasn't looking? He clutches these thoughts, cold in the pit of his stomach, as a sharp wind tangles in his hair.

"I can't believe it," Reed murmurs, voice cracking like the ice below their feet. "An unwitting killer. Was it really me?" His words hang, a breath of mist trembling in the silence before the mountains swallow them whole.

Miranda watches him, as though she might map out his burden in her gaze. Her empathy for him is profound, not spoken but felt in the shared silences between their words—the things they do not say. Reed is a shade of her own struggle, each line of his face a mirror of her own haunted reflection. No answers are offered, only a quiet refuge in shared agony.

"It's hard to recognize yourself after something like this," Miranda offers, her voice firm but gentle, like the cracking of thawing ice. "We were dragged under by forces we didn't understand, Reed."

For a moment, they stand suspended between worlds: beneath a cavernous sky that teeters between breaking and dawn. Everything feels fragile now, emotions jangling with the same uncertainty as the wind whispering through the alpine pines.

Reed draws a breath, tries to reconcile the person standing here with the one he thought he was—a foolishness, maybe, to think knowledge could be so easily layered over years of conditioned loyalty. And yet, there it is: a scorching light of truth that reveals everything in stark relief. Perhaps there is freedom in choosing to define oneself anew.

"I guess it's about moving forward now," he suggests, the hint of determination mixing with trepidation in his tone. "Finding out who we're going to be."

Miranda nods, the slightest motion of solidarity, and they turn their gazes away from the wreckage to face the path ahead. They find some balance in the other's steady presence, the reflection of shared battles in the other's eyes. The Alps spread majestic and serene around them, a world untouched by their burdens, promising unknown trails shrouded in mist.

In this stillness, as frost glistens quietly beneath twilight, they understand what survival demands: that they piece together what remains, towards whatever horizon tomorrow presents. The solace lies not in the quietude, but in the strength of moving forward side by side, even as shadows of past and future stretch interminably before them.

Conclave of Deception

In the low-lit confines of a secure meeting room in Washington D.C., whispers weave like serpents among high-ranking intelligence officials. Their voices, practiced in discretion, murmur about Project Morpheus and The Warden's activities. Leaning in under the guise of confidentiality, they deliberate, afraid of the chaos truths could unleash on an unsuspecting public. Nods spread like ripples across the room, a silent agreement to bury the evidence deep beneath the heavy drapes of national security.

The officials' commitment to secrecy reflects an entrenched political strategy: curbing transparency to maintain the fragile illusion of control. The shadows of previous governmental subterfuges linger in the room, echoing a time-honored tradition of safeguarding order over truth. In the broader scheme, their maneuvers are acts of protection, however flawed, shielding the populace from the ricocheting terror that unchecked revelation might provoke.

Beyond the cloak-and-dagger conversations, within the cracks of protocol, stands Miranda—unseen yet present. Her ears catch fragments of their discourse, each word a weighted stone tossed into her pool of unease. Her brow furrows, an external marker of internal storm. A conflict festers within: the public's right to know balanced against the potential upheavals that transparency might ignite.

Miranda's mind churns with the moral ambiguity of their clandestine plans. The conversation loops in her head, growing louder, drowning out reason. Could it be justified to suppress a past haunted by cyclical violence, in pursuit of a peace built upon lies? Or is it a moral imperative to thrust this narrative, raw and dangerous, into the glaring light?

Silently, she retreats from the scene, the weight of their secrecy pressing heavier than the Swiss Alps' blanket of snow. The serenity of her alpine experiences contrasts sharply with the barbed wire of deception that coils tighter around her conscience. Her steps are measured, away from the meeting room, understanding the labyrinth of choice she now navigates. As the shadows wrap around her, she realizes that the cost of buried truths may be higher than any chaos truth could evoke.

Echoes of Regret

The hotel room is dim and cloaked in silence, shadows weaving across the walls like whispers of his past. Reed sits alone, his gaze fixed unwaveringly on the blank expanse before him, as if challenging it to reveal the truths he's fled from for too long. His mind is a tumult of images—faces, places, actions; all blurring together in a disconcerting dance of memory and remorse.

Determined to reclaim his narrative, Reed reaches for a notebook. His hand trembles slightly as ink spills across the page. The pen scratches methodically, tracing the contours of recollections just out of reach. Each stroke of the pen is a command, a plea for clarity amidst the wreckage of his thoughts. He seeks the outline of his past —missions cloaked in shadow, decisions made under the weight of The Warden's influence. Distorted, yet unmistakable, the visions come and go, leaving him momentarily breathless.

The door opens with a quiet click, and Miranda steps inside the dimly lit space, her presence a balm to his agitation. She approaches silently, her footsteps soft against the plush carpet, her aura of calm a constant amidst his internal storm. It's not the words she offers but the simple act of being there that conveys understanding; the bond between them has been forged through shared trials, understanding deeper than the ghosts haunting his conscience.

Reed puts the pen down, his voice heavy with an uncertainty that seems foreign to him. "I don't know who

I am anymore," he admits, the words raw as they cut through the quiet. The notebook lies open between them, emblematic of his restless confusion, a collection of thoughts suspended precariously, like loose pages on the verge of fluttering away.

Miranda steps closer, placing a reassuring hand on his shoulder. The simple contact anchors him, a connection amidst the swirling doubts that threaten to take him under. In her touch, he senses the quiet echo of shared anguish, of paths both dark and uncertain. She gives no answers, makes no promises, yet in that moment, their solidarity speaks louder than any assurance could. They stand together, an unspoken vow to confront whatever future may bring, determined to forge light from the shadows of their past.

Reflections of Resolve

Miranda stands at the hotel room window, her breath fogging the glass momentarily. Beyond, the Zurich skyline sprawls out like a glittering puzzle against the night. The city's lights flicker, merging with her reflection, casting shadows that dance across her face—half in shadow, half in light. Her gaze drifts away from the shimmering glow, delving into the recesses of her memories where the weight of Project Morpheus still clings like cobwebs refusing to be swept away. Each flicker of the skyline is a ghost of her past—an indistinct image from her time entwined in a world crafted by manipulation and control.

In the dim light of their hotel room, echoes of Miranda's past intrude, unbidden, wrapping around her like tendrils of smoke. She envisions the sterile laboratories, the cold glint of surgical steel, and The Warden's voice—a voice that had once seemed like the hand guiding her destiny. Those days were a fever dream of lost autonomy, a pseudo-existence masquerading as purpose. The experimental thrall of being an operative had twisted her sense of self, leaving gaping wounds that the soft kisses of healing could, only in time, soothe. Her participation in the psychological experiments had been a dance of deceit, clashing with the reality she now sought to claim —one filtered free from others' agendas. The Warden's image haunts her still, the reminder that she had existed in that purgatorial world, between freedom and bondage.

A steely resolve begins to surface, solidifying through the vapor of old memories. It is time to liberate herself from the specters of her history, to craft a narrative where her voice reigns supreme and unchallenged. Her path will be hers alone, unfettered by the invisible chains that sought to bind and control. Her reflection stares back, a vessel filled with newfound strength, jaw set in determination. She resolves to weave her legacy, steadfast in her decision to resist becoming another cog in a shadowy machine; her agency a beacon in the swirling haze of her recollections.

The atmosphere is imbued with an introspective silence as Miranda steps back from the window, the cityscape imprinting its rhythm onto her soul. The room's low light mirrors her newly embraced path. Her thoughts clear and unwavering, she turns away from the glass, leaving behind the reflections of her past to forge ahead into the light of self-determination. She strides with purpose, embraced by the resolve that binds her heart and mind.

The Resurgence Cipher

The evening settles over Zurich like a heavy blanket, the hotel room dimly lit by the streetlight filtering through the curtains. Miranda sinks into the worn leather chair by the window, her fatigue palpable, when her phone vibrates softly against the table. Her heart quickens, intuition whispering that this message would not bring comfort. She hesitates, fingers hovering over the screen, before opening the encrypted text.

"You cannot erase an idea. Morpheus was only the beginning."

The stark words are icy tendrils curling around her spine. The message is a ghostly whisper from the past—one she thought she'd left behind. The room seems to narrow around her, shadows closing in like dark waves against a fragile vessel. Instead of clarity, the words sow unease, probing at fears she's fought hard to suppress. What is this resurgence? Will she forever live under the shadow of Morpheus?

A chill courses through her. Survival has carved resolve into her bones, yet she's not blind to reality: Morpheus was not buried deep enough. The idea is a disease, relentless and spreading, with her as its unwilling carrier. How easily can freedom unravel when past horrors resurface? She closes her eyes, grappling with the potential that their fight might only have scratched the surface.

"Reed," she calls, voice steady despite the turmoil within. He comes to her side, expression weary yet attentive, as she shows him the text. Words are unnecessary; their shared glance communicates all they need. They had believed in brief respite, a pause in a battle long fought, but the message is a bitter reminder. Victory, if it could be called that, was only a temporary truce. Their war rages on.

“We have to keep going,” she says finally, eyes fixed on Reed’s, searching for mutual understanding, determination to match hers. Their adversities have forged an unspoken bond, and in this moment, that connection is their North Star. Whether it leads them to ruin or salvation, only time will tell.

Reed nods, features resolving into determination honed by shared trials. “Then we plan,” he replies, a man accustomed to clarity in chaos. “But we need to outmaneuver what we can’t outfight.”

In silent agreement, they pour over maps and files, sifting through clues and patterns in the dim light. Strategies form like pieces of a restless dream, the kind that slips away in the morning. Their voices meld with the city’s nocturnal symphony, footsteps in the hall, distant traffic. They are two soldiers in an unwelcome war.

Through it all, questions linger like smoke that refuses to settle. Miranda’s thoughts wander: What shape will this new threat take? What if the next attack is one they can’t anticipate? The possibilities gnaw at her resolve, yet the potential for change—real change—spurs her onward. If they are to face this shadowy foe once more, it must be with the same courage that brought them here.

Eventually, the city hushes in the early hours, and Reed closes the last map. They sit in the quiet, plans suspended in the air between them like whispered promises, fragility and determination in equal measure. New threats may sleep among them, waiting to awaken, but they will meet whatever comes with open eyes and steady hearts. Together, they face the dark as a pact is silently renewed, an unyielding bond forged in the crucible of their shared struggle.

Crossroads of Identity

Outside the hotel, the dim light of the alleyway casts long shadows that merge with the night. Miranda stands there, her breath forming small clouds in the chilly air as she eyes a figure approaching. Her contact is almost indistinguishable from the alley's obscurity, a person who speaks in whispers of new beginnings and erased pasts. The promise is alluring—vanish everything that binds her to the nightmare of Project Morpheus and step into a fresh existence.

She hesitates, grappling with thoughts that swirl like shadows around her mind. Freedom, identity—intangible concepts that seem both so close and yet elusive. What does it mean to be truly free? To scrub away the fragments of oneself that define the core of who she is? Each life holds darkness and light, the depth of one's identity perhaps rooted in what they overcome rather than what they erase. Memories flood back—each harrowing experience tied to Morpheus, each scar a testament to survival. Miranda wonders if she can live with the disconnect of forgetting who she was and what she's been through. Yet, the longing for escape, the chance to unshackle from the past's weight, tugs at her heart, leaving her in a realm of uncertainty.

“We can make it so you were never here,” the contact says softly, their voice weaving through the alley like a thread through a needle. The offer lingers, a tempting whisper of liberation.

Miranda draws a breath, searching her reflection in the contact's eyes, seeking answers in the frail light. Just then, Reed steps into the gloom, his presence grounding her. He doesn’t need to say much; it’s his calm certainty that speaks volumes. Despite his own burdens, Reed stands there, a reminder of resilience and the fight they’ve shared.

“You can find new purpose, Miranda. It’s in you,” he murmurs, voice steady amid echoes of resolve.

She feels a warmth spreading from his words, seeping into the fractures of her doubt. Strength had always been there, nestled beneath layers of trauma, a quiet flame nurtured through shared battles and quiet nights of introspection. Reed’s reminder acts like a beacon—a call to embrace the essence within that was forged through trials and tribulations.

Her mind flits back to the alleyway’s promise, comparing it to the steadfastness of Reed’s conviction. A life without the anchors of the past might seem lighter but is it truly what she desires? Miranda stares at the abyss of choices laid before her and senses a burgeoning clarity. It’s the stories we carry, the scars and triumphs, that knit the fabric of our resilience and unmistakably shape the journey forward.

Turning away from the contact, she faces Reed, feeling the weight of her decision settle with calming finality.

The alley seems brighter—a path clear, her resolve toughened by everything she's seen and survived.

Reed grasps it without needing any more words exchanged, their understanding an unspoken bond that has grown beyond shared hardships. With a quick nod, she's acknowledging the ally she has in him, the horizons she now strives toward not alone but together.

Together, they step back toward the hotel, each footfall finding solace in decision, the world around them gradually shifting into sharper focus.

CHAPTER 15

THE SLEEPWALKER'S CURSE

The Price of Oblivion

Miranda sits at the far corner of the dimly lit café in Zurich, her eyes tracing the rivulets of rain streaming down the windowpane—a world beyond, both alien and familiar. Across from her, a man shrouded in shadows leans forward, his offer a mere whisper among the clinks and clatter of cutlery and hurried voices.

"This could erase it all, you know," he murmurs, sliding a small file across the table, its edges curling like the remnants of an old photograph. "Every trace of who you were, gone. You're sure this is what you want?"

She picks at the state-issued napkin, the weight of his words hanging heavily between them. Can she really erase the specters of Project Morpheus? Would shedding her skin be any more freeing than a snake discarding its old scales, only to reveal a freshly vulnerable layer?

In the dim light, her thoughts churn. The night's solitude presses in on her, mingling with memories she can never fully unravel. Traumatic visions dance behind her eyelids—flashes of rooms unfamiliar and yet so intrinsically tied to her understanding of self. Rooms shrouded in sterile lights, endless cycles of waking dreams, and the thin line between mending and manipulation.

"What's the price?" Her voice cracks just slightly, betraying the internal maelstrom.

"Identity, for one. Everyone who knew you—even the you that knew you—could be lost." His gaze doesn't waver, eyes hidden behind the gleam of technical promises and perceived freedom.

She considers this, her mind retracing paths of peril and woe. Faces, names, events spiraling like a tempest—each a thread in the tapestry of who she'd been forced to become. The project had demanded sacrifices, had sculpted her into something both terrifying and deceptively human.

She flickers between worlds, each foot grounded in its own reality. Does she genuinely own any of herself, or is each heartbeat a metronome counting down to oblivion?

"I... need time," she admits, her resolve obscuring the fissure of fear. "Just one step—I can't shed it all right now."

Thoughts clash within her like lightning against the slow rumble of distant thunder. To truly forget would mean to reject any morsel of understanding that could redeem her, though she knows deliverance remains cagey. Even from this exile existence, she is not truly free.

The contact nods, tucking the file back into the folds of his coat as their dialogue dissipates into the café's muted hum. Patrons float in a dance of whispered conversations, cups raised in communion with shared frailty.

As the rain continues its descent, Miranda is left to ponder the torn threads of identity and agency that entangle her. Here, caught between hope clashing with fear, she remains a mosaic of everything she was, and everything she fears she'll never escape.

The Awakening of the Sleeper

In the hushed stillness of a suburban night, a faint buzzing stirs an unsuspecting quiet. In one of the quaint cookie-cutter homes, dimly lit by a single streetlight, a phone resting on the corner of a neat oak desk vibrates. Its signal is a silent invocation, unnoticed by the world outside where crickets serenade the evening air.

The device hums again, and a man lets his gaze stray from a book he is pretending to read—a spine-creased paperback about the joys of gardening. He lifts the phone to eye level, face illuminated in a sterile blue hue. His pupils dilate as the message unfolds, wiring its insidious power directly into his consciousness.

In an instant, the casual veneer of the reader transforms, flesh taut over sculpted planes like a statue brought to life with unholy precision. His eyes, now piercing and unyielding, carve a path through the shadows. This shift, subtle and chilling, reveals a latent identity crafted from covert machinations.

He moves with purpose, his actions devoid of hesitation. Within a shallow closet behind untouched suits in shades of gray and navy, he retrieves the gear of a different facet of his reality: a compact handgun, a sleek knife with a blade glinting maliciously in the dim light, and a garrote wire resting carefully in a velvet pouch. Each object holds a promise of precision, a potent testament to its dormant purpose.

His heart beats steadily, in deadly rhythm with the dormant part of his psyche that has just surged awake. It's as if a layer of dust has been swept away, revealing machinery oiled and well-maintained beneath the mundane facade of his orderly life.

As the agent crosses the threshold of his home, the cozy suburban interior gives way to the vast unknown. The night envelopes him, cool and indifferent, while his calculated footsteps carry him deeper into shadow. The street, once innocuous, seems to shrink, swallowed by the encroaching darkness.

In that moment, the illusion of the suburban idyll fractures. The world teeters on the precipice of potential chaos—an ecosystem infiltrated by the agents of Project Morpheus who lie in wait, stationed inside society's very structures.

Yet, to any observer in a passing car or peering through half-drawn blinds, nothing seems amiss. Still, in the pitch of night, the silhouettes move with calculated intent. Soon, perhaps, the network of normalcy will unravel.

With each step, the sleeper agent delves deeper into his role, mission unfolding like an old record, etched into his mind with chilling clarity. This is not just a shadowed path of destruction but an orchestrated advance in a game where the rules are dictated by unseen powers—the dark hands shaping the world's axis, turning unnoticed until it is too late.

As the agent disappears into the thick of night, his figure swallows the last vestiges of light. What began in quiet suburbia becomes an aperture of estrangement—a landscape consumed by impending threat, where the sleeper's presence signifies an omen of unrest.

And with that, the darkness closes in, an impenetrable cloak swallowing any hint of his passage, whispering promises of the latent chaos couched in the ordinary.

Embers of Redemption

Reed sits across from Miranda on the soft, worn couch in their safe house. The room is dimly lit, accented only by the glow of a solitary table lamp. His expression betrays a storm of emotions, swirling with both trust and doubt. Miranda's gaze shifts to him, attuned to the weight he carries, an understanding borne out of shared battles. She knows the chaos that still etches lines on his face, the shadows that dance in his eyes, remnants of fragmented memories.

As Reed speaks, his words hover in the air, acknowledging the trust he still holds for her, tangled with the echoes of his programming. Conversations occur that suggest there's a history secure enough to anchor them both, despite the trembling ground beneath. He leans forward, his posture a signal of determination—a stark reminder that fleeing from their past isn't the resolution they seek.

Miranda nods, feeling a pang of empathy twist within her. She thinks about how Reed's struggle reflects her own tangled emotions. Her hands twitch slightly as she ponders the scars Project Morpheus has left on her — moments where her instincts were her enemy, where her own identity betrayed her. The thought sends a chill creeping up her spine, but she pushes it aside, focusing on Reed with a resolve that steadies her heartbeat.

"Running won't solve anything," Reed insists. His voice is firm, yet betrays an undercurrent of vulnerability, exposing frayed nerves and an uncertain heart.

Miranda reaches out, taking his hand gently. Her touch anchors them both to the here and now, cutting through the confusion their twisted pasts have sown. Her words come softly but they carry a promise: "We can overcome this, Reed. We're not defined by what they made us. We can rise beyond those chains."

For a moment, silence engulfs the room—a silence thick with an unspoken bond, a pact forged from trials too numerous to count. Her mind swirls with flashes from a different life—one dictated by another's command—and she wonders if Reed battles similar ghosts. The memories are like frayed edges of a tapestry she cannot mend, woven with fear of becoming a specter of her own past.

Their mutual pledge forms between them in the shadowed corners of the room, an understanding without words. It doesn't matter how turbulent the road ahead is, nor how haunting their memories. It's their shared commitment, a fragile yet defiant flicker in the darkness.

In this moment, their understanding is complete; a resolve cast in the dim lamplight that illuminates the truth—past shackles can be broken, demons faced. As they sit, the room hums with life that reaches out for redemption, drawing two battered souls together against the remnants of Project Morpheus. Together, they will face the fears clawing at the corners of their existence, choosing to stand resilient and unyielding against an uncertain dawn.

Unchained Resolve

In the dim light of her safe house bedroom, shadows danced across the walls, swelling and contracting like the doubts that plagued Miranda Carter. The thrum of her heart quickened as her phone vibrated, a single message appearing: encrypted, familiar, chilling. The Warden's insidious echo lingered within the simple words, reverberating through her consciousness, stirring memories of whispered promises and binding chains. She sat frozen, staring at the cryptic text, her mind a tempest of fear and defiance.

The weight of her identity pressed heavily upon her shoulders, reminiscent of the burden she'd carried for so long. What did freedom look like without the specter of control shadowing her each step? She had played roles she never auditioned for, a pawn in a game whose rules she never learned. The Warden's influence curled around her thoughts, taunting her with the shimmering illusion of choice. If she had been part of his chessboard, could she break free, or was she doomed to remain a piece, forever moved by unseen hands?

Doubts whispered insidiously, weaving tales of inadequacy and futility. Could she possess the strength to redefine her fate, to seize control from those who had wielded her like a weapon? Memories flooded back—glimpses of sterile halls and the cold eyes of observers, documenting each action, each whisper of rebellion suppressed before it could blossom. The burden of her past pressed heavily upon her, old wounds reopening with sudden, searing familiarity. Yet beneath the doubt, a flicker of resolve sparked.

The room was cast in the soft luminescence of a nearby lamp, its glow suffusing the darkness with a promise—as if the very light defied the looming shadows. Miranda reached into herself, encountering deep wells of courage previously untapped. The Warden might have cast her into the abyss, but she could climb out, unshackled. She inhaled deeply, the decision solidifying in her chest. Resolve tempered like steel, she would confront and dismantle the remnants of her past, embracing an agency long denied.

With the determination to fight back burning within, she silenced the doubts, acknowledging her scars not as evidence of brokenness but as emblems of survival. As the flickering shadows receded, giving way to a stronger, unwavering light, Miranda's resolve crystallized. True independence was within her reach. She stood, gathering herself against the chill of the night, ready to face whatever lay beyond the safe house walls.

Threshold of a New Dawn

The first light of dawn creeps through the thin curtains of the safe house, casting long shadows that stretch ominously across the floor. Miranda Carter stands in the somber stillness, the cool handle of the front door under her fingers like a tether to reality. Beyond this threshold lies an uncertain world, alive with both potential freedom and unseen threats.

As she pauses, The Warden's lingering influence presses heavily on her—a specter of past manipulations that refuse to fade. She knows that erasing her history might offer solace, a clean slate, yet it means severing the last threads of her true self. Memories flash—bitter rehearsals of The Warden's games, the labyrinthine corridors where she once wandered, not as an investigator but as a tool. Who would she be without these scars, without this burden of knowing the darkest recesses of human control?

Hope mingles with instinctual dread. What if the darkness of her past is necessary to reclaim her future? Drawing strength from the idea, she understands that even shadows offer clarity in their stark contrast against the light. Embracing them could mean reclaiming power over her own destiny, redirecting fear into a blade sharpened against those who would pull her strings.

Reed had once said, "We carry pieces of who we were as shields, not chains." His words echo now as she draws a deep breath, her resolve crystallizing into a difficult clarity. Stepping into the cool morning air, the chill kisses her skin like a whispered promise of a new beginning or an end to her nightmares.

"Maybe I never woke up," she murmurs, each syllable hanging in the air like mist before a rising sun. A paradox of her own making—one that suggests she might always be part of the game, but one she will redefine on her terms.

As the door closes securely behind her, the city awaits. Her path remains tangled and treacherous, yet her steps are firm and unyielding in this dawn's fragile light. Ready to wrestle with whatever specter of Morpheus dares linger at her horizon.

Epilogue

The War Isn't Over

In a shadowed corner of a dim Zürich café, Miranda watches rain trace the window as a mysterious figure slides a weathered file toward her. His hushed offer promises to wipe away every remnant of her past with Project Morpheus—as if shedding an old skin to reveal a vulnerable new self. Torn between liberation and the loss of every memory that once defined her, she murmurs, "I need time." As the contact vanishes into the café's muted hum, she remains with a heavy heart, questioning whether true freedom lies in forgetting or in bearing the scars.

On a silent suburban night, a phone's subtle buzz disrupts the calm of an ordinary home. A man, once lost in a gardening book, suddenly transforms. His eyes harden as a cryptic message unlocks a hidden persona. From a closet of untouched suits, he retrieves a compact handgun, knife, and garrote—a precise arsenal summoned by a dormant force. Stepping out into the enveloping darkness, his figure slips away, leaving behind the comforting illusion of suburbia for a path destined to sow chaos.

In the soft glow of a safe house, Reed sits on a worn couch, burdened by fragmented memories and unspoken guilt. Miranda's gentle presence bridges the silence as they share a quiet, resolute conversation. "Running won't solve anything," he confesses, his voice a mix of vulnerability and determination. As she clasps his hand, their mutual pledge to rise above the chains of Project Morpheus lights a spark of hope—a fragile but defiant promise to reclaim their true selves.

Call of the Unseen

In a serene suburban living room, a solitary figure drifts through nostalgia—until an urgent phone message shatters the stillness: "It's time to wake up." Stirred from his reverie, he discovers a hidden briefcase tucked away behind an oak cabinet—a relic of secret purpose. With newfound resolve, he steps into the night, merging with the shadows as the familiar street dissolves behind him, leaving the quiet neighborhood unchanged but his destiny forever altered.

.... THE END ....

BACK MATTER

About the Author

Lena Lexington weaves tales that defy the boundaries of reality and delve deep into the labyrinth of the human mind. With a passion for psychological suspense and intricate storytelling, Lena invites you to explore the darkest corners of the soul through narratives that are as vibrant as they are haunting. *Hypnotized Assassin* is her latest plunge into a world where memory, identity, and control blur into one relentless thriller.

Author's Note

Thank you for venturing into the shadowy realms of *Hypnotized Assassin* . This story was born from a desire to challenge perceptions and ignite the imagination. Every twist, every secret, and every moment of suspense is an invitation to question the nature of free will and the fragility of memory. As you close these pages, I hope you carry with you the thrill of discovery and the spark of curiosity that fuels our inner journey.

Connect & Share

Your thoughts and insights are incredibly valuable. If *Hypnotized Assassin* resonated with you, please consider leaving a review. Let your voice be heard—each review helps to illuminate the path for future readers and fuels the creative spirit behind every story.

Stay connected for updates on future projects and behind-the-scenes insights by visiting my website or following me on social media.

Thank you for reading. May the echoes of the shadows inspire your next great adventure.

Lena Lexington Mar 2025 Bangkok

Dawn of Triumph

Shadows quake at dawn's first cry,

Secrets unravel where fear used to lie.

A traitor unmasked, illusions undone,

Justice stands tall beneath the rising sun.

In the hush of triumph, new hope takes flight,

Darkness recedes, yielding to radiant light.

Made in the USA
Las Vegas, NV
01 April 2025

e481e0b0-cfef-44bc-9e89-aacbe558302fR01